advance praise for
THE SECRET SKIN

"Blends the vivid DNA of *Rebecca* and *Jane Eyre* with a glorious, muscular queer magnificence that is all Wendy's own. Sexy, scary, compelling, incredible."
—Sam J. Miller, Nebula Award-winning author of *Blackfish City*

"A deeply compelling tale of family, secrets, betrayal and love at all costs. *The Secret Skin* caught me in its gothic spell, and kept me turning pages into the witching hours."
—Nebula Award-winning author Kelly Robson

"A beautifully written piece of gothic horror, suffused with all the peculiarities of the 1920s in coastal Oregon. Pitch perfect language combines with the brilliant decision to make our narrator both the governess and the inheritor of the manor, a masterful twist on genre tropes."
—Caitlin Starling, author of *The Death of Jane Lawrence*

"*The Secret Skin* is kind of what might happen if you crossed 'The Fall of the House of Usher' with *Rebecca*, supplemented the result with a child with supernatural powers, and transported it all to the Pacific Northwest. A lively, wild novella, with a nice dark edge to it."
—Brian Evenson, author of *A Collapse of Horses* and *The Warren*

"Wagner's eerie, gorgeously rendered tale goes all in on gothic decadence...The evocative prose and insightful heroine make this a treasure."
—Publishers Weekly

"Perfect for reading on a rainy night, *Rebecca* meets *The Turn of the Screw* in this jewel-box of a novella by Wendy Wagner."
—Molly Tanzer, author of *Creatures of Will and Temper*

Neon Hemlock Press
www.neonhemlock.com
@neonhemlock

The Secret Skin
Wendy N. Wagner

This novella is entirely a work of fiction. Names,
characters, places and incidents are the products of
the author's imagination or are used fictitiously. Any
resemblance to actual events, locales, organizations or
persons, living or dead, is entirely coincidental.

Cover Illustration by Bailie Rosenlund
Cover Design by dave ring

Paperback ISBN-13: 978-1-952086-32-8
Ebook ISBN-13: 978-1-952086-29-8

Wendy N. Wagner
THE SECRET SKIN

Neon Hemlock Press

THE 2021 NEON HEMLOCK NOVELLA SERIES

NEON HEMLOCK

The Secret Skin

BY WENDY N. WAGNER

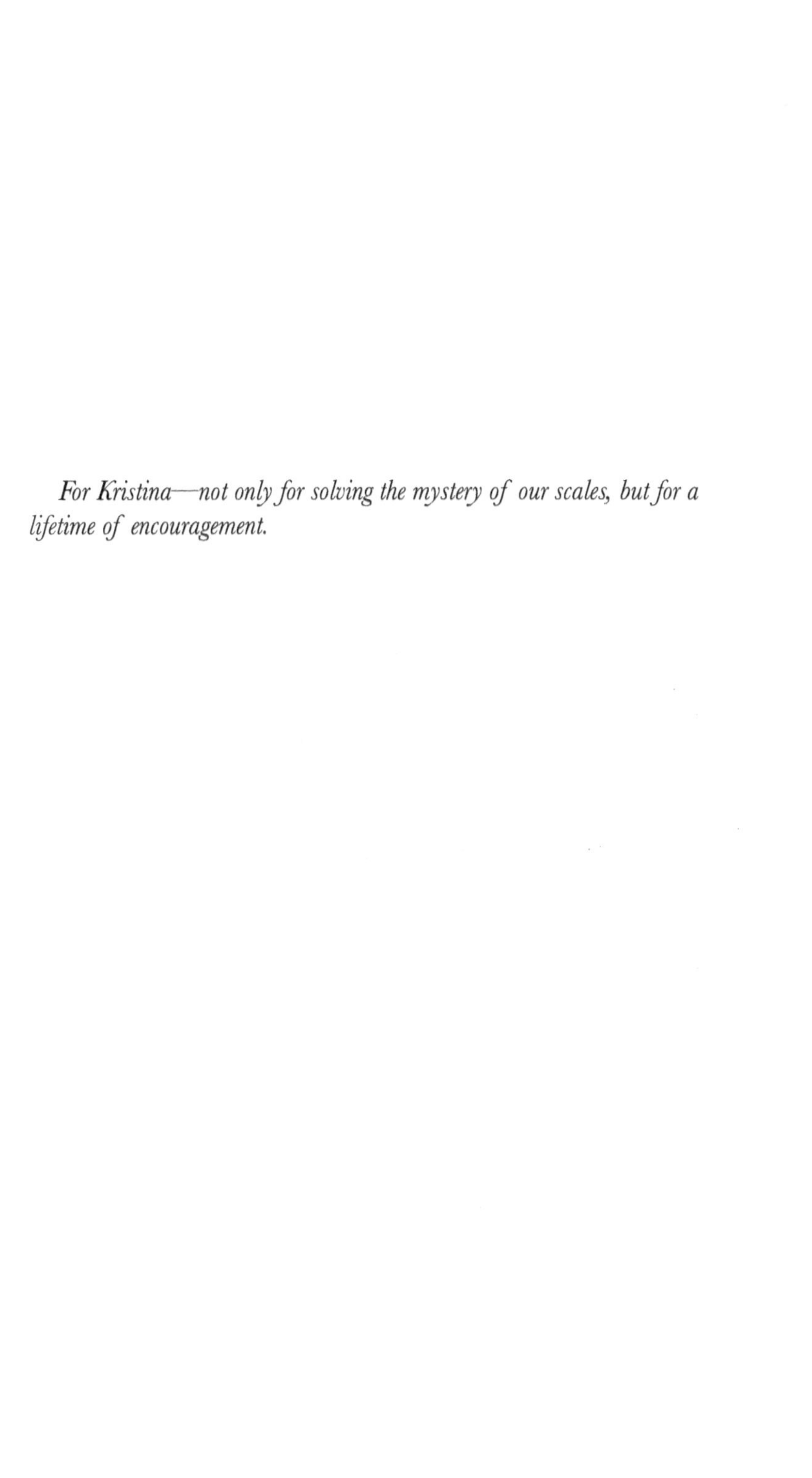

For Kristina—not only for solving the mystery of our scales, but for a lifetime of encouragement.

L AST NIGHT I dreamed of Storm Break, dear Lillian, for the first time since we escaped that salt place. Neither you nor Abigail stood beside me. I was alone, an invisible witness, a pair of eyes suspended in the mist.

Down the front driveway I came, sweeping over the moon-white length of crushed oyster shells, and in my dream the house was not the place I said goodbye to that night with the roses clawing at our legs, but instead the house of my childhood, all lit up for one of Maman's parties. Servants moved past me in the sweet spring night, their coattails swinging as they hurried to meet the guests in their motor-cars. The dream figures were sometimes Frederick and sometimes Beamon, and sometimes they were somehow both.

The sounds, though, were perfect. You don't realize how much the sounds make a time or a place. Storm Break in its heyday had its own pattern of sounds. Always, somewhere, there was an engine: the snarl of someone's Mercedes or the smooth growl of one of my father's boats. Day or night there was always some reason to run a motor, much to Daddy's joy. On the far side of the grounds, the horses made their own funny music, a counterpoint to the constant tinkling laughter of the guests.

And always the sea. You remember that, Lil. Sometimes I wake in the night missing the sound of it, and only you can sing me back to sleep.

If there was one reason to go back to Storm Break, it would be to stand on the great cliff and watch and listen to the endless murmuring motion of the waves.

But I cannot. That house, as we knew it, is gone.

I was born in Storm Break, and I very nearly died in it. On the worst nights, the nights when the trains make an endless screeching, or Abigail wakes in one of her fits, or I've been drinking too much bootleg whiskey: on those nights I think perhaps I should have died there. But some nights—most nights, Lillian—I lie in your arms and I try not to think about Storm Break except to be glad that I have seen the last of it.

It was built and it lived and it died, that house. It awakened to the kind of life that only living things can know, for it was a great house, the first of its kind in its wild place. And like all great houses, it breathed in secrets and whispered them in the dark.

The ones I know, I'm writing this letter to explain to you. The ones I don't?

Well, I suppose that they, like Storm Break, remain the province of the wind, and the waves, and the things that watch beneath the ragged petals of the roses.

ONE

A PASSENGER TRAIN ran from Portland to Coos Bay, but given
my family, it was cheaper to catch one of our steamers
headed south. The ships didn't usually put in on the route from
Grays Harbor to San Francisco, but for my brother, they made
an exception. That's how it was when you were a Vogel. There
were bigger ship-builders and richer lumber companies, but my
family did well enough.

That was only a year ago, but it feels much longer, sitting here
in our little set of rooms. Mrs. Hendricks, the headmistress at the
ladies academy, rode with me to the river boat that would take
me from Portland to the coast. We didn't talk much, but that
suited me. We'd never been close, my employer and I, but we
both knew I had no desire to return to my family's estate. At the
docks, she gave me a new pair of gloves; Joseph, our driver and
handyman gave me a stiff, whiskery hug that nearly knocked off
my cloche hat. I couldn't remember the last time someone had
hugged me. Not even my pupils were much inclined.

If anyone in my family had ever hugged me, I suppose it was Frederick. Of all my siblings, he spent the most time at the family's Oregon habitation. We were the closest in age, although he had a good ten years on me, and we both had my mother's skin. It made him shy as a boy, all his scales showing beneath his short pants, but once they were hidden away, he became as friendly and delightful as a golden retriever.

People said he took after my mother that way. She was known from Seattle to Sacramento for her gracious ways and wonderful parties. Being gracious is not the same as being friendly, or kind, or loving, but it counts a very great deal inside the Portland-San Francisco-Southern Oregon social circles that my mother ran in.

That my mother *dominated*. Despite its location in the most backwater of Oregon's backwaters, Storm Break had hosted three governors, a half-dozen senators, and an entire fleet of local officials during her tenure as hostess, and after her passing, Frederick's wife Blanche had kept up the house's good reputation.

Things had gone quiet since Blanche died eight years ago. It wasn't that Frederick didn't enjoy a good party, but his schedule kept him too busy for a social life—or so I presumed from his letters. I re-read the latest several times during my journey down the coast. He had filled it with his customary happy dashes of business and charity work and only just managed to squeeze in the itinerary for his honeymoon. His letters were so chatty I had actually missed the fact he'd gotten engaged. I might have never realized he'd remarried if he hadn't begun discussing plans for a lavish honeymoon spent traveling in Mexico.

Two months he'd be gone. Two months, that if I didn't mind horribly, if I could oh please, for the sake of family feeling, set aside my summer plans and help out with his little girl, such a good girl no matter what the last nanny said. Such a lonely little girl who couldn't be left alone in a house filled with servants, not when she could learn firsthand what family really meant.

Looking back, Lil, I am surprised I succumbed to my brother's pleading. But maybe I was looking for some excuse, any excuse, to face my family pile one more time—to see it with fresh eyes, to say goodbye, maybe, to the people who had died under its roof.

I supposed that in two months' time there'd be someone else making the rules at Storm Break. A new wife, a new chance for a Vogel heir, a new excuse for a party. Prohibition or not, my brother deserved a big party. He had been through dark times those past eight years. So much loss, and a little girl to raise, too.

I never once thought I needed to see Abigail. If I had spent time with her during that last year at home, I could not remember any interactions in any detail. I did remember her eyes, wide and brown as my own when I was a little thing, and I have a few sketches of her in the sketchbook I managed to bring away with me when I left Storm Break. But I know I never changed a diaper or fed Abigail, and I don't remember ever holding her. I imagine I wasn't allowed to. Blanche had so many rules about her baby.

Some feeling squirmed within me, and I pulled out my sketchbook and pencil. Storm Break was not far now. Those rocks to the south of us had to mark the tip of Cape Arago. My hand moved over the page, following my eyes as they scrolled across the sky. But as we went around the cliffs beneath Storm Break, I put my pencil in the sketchbook and closed my eyes. I wasn't ready to see the estate yet. Better to prepare myself by the long ride up the harbor road. Better to let the crushed oyster drive slowly reveal the house—the house that workers had finished on the very day I was born within its walls.

We were a strange sort of twins, Storm Break and I. I half yearned to be under its roof and half yearned to wing like a seabird back up the coast, back to my room in Mrs. Shavington's boarding house, my students, my paintings, my friends. I couldn't imagine spending the summer with a spoiled nine-year-old girl.

The wind softened as the ship began its slow slide toward Charleston. The air smelled of ferns and fish guts, and the boats we passed were filled with eyes staring back at me, the faces raw with interest. It was the same expression people had been making at me my entire childhood, and seeing it, I felt as if I hadn't merely traveled two hundred miles south, but also back in time. The world looked younger here, the people far removed from the cultural and scientific advances of Oregon's biggest city.

I felt younger here. If I opened my mouth, the voice that emerged would be tinged with the proper Victorian tones my mother had devoted herself to cultivating.

With a splash, the deep-water steamer dropped anchor at the mouth of the harbor. It could go no farther. My father had ordered it built too big for the bay beside his own home.

The crew put me out in a dinghy, the two sailors mooring for a moment at the docks and then whisking away with only a deferent touch of their hats. There was no one on the dock to meet me.

I sat myself upon my trunk and wondered how I'd ever get to the house. It was ten miles from Charleston to the tiny town of Yarrow, and three more straight uphill to Storm Break. I couldn't be sure Charleston even had a telephone line yet.

"Miss Vogel? Miss June Vogel?" The words stretched themselves like syrup melting down a stack of hot pancakes.

I turned away from the water to face the man with the southern vowels. I didn't recognize his face, round and sun-stained beneath an extensive forehead, framed in the least appealing fashion by a few threads of pomaded hair. Oil glistened on his mustache, and his suit looked newer than most. Whoever he was, he had some little money, and he knew my face. In this part of the coast, that meant he worked for my family.

I sat taller. "I'm Miss Vogel."

"How fine to see you, young lady."

I found the words my mother would have used. "It's been so long since I've been home, everyone's a stranger." She would have smiled at this point in the conversation, so I tried to, as well. "You are?"

He put out a grasping claw with moist flesh. "Ebenezer Watson. I'm the manager at the sawmill these days. I also help Frederick run the estate."

Frederick, not *Mr. Vogel*. Oh, I knew his type. Reaching, always reaching. I knew that if I put out my gloved hand, he would crush it in his grip as if to show me just how much a man he really was.

I held out my suitcase instead. "I'm so glad Mr. Vogel arranged for my transit. And with such a high-placed associate. Shall we be off?" I glanced over my shoulder. "I do have a trunk, as you can see."

I did not see his face go sour, but I felt his posture change. Men who reach above their stations take any slight with a fierce bitterness. I swept down the dock without a backward glance. If I was back in Portland, I could have never managed the imperious set of my shoulders, the lifted chin. Back there, I was a nobody. An art teacher in a private girls' school who dabbled in painting portraits on the side. But here I was a Vogel. I could act like one for a summer, anyway.

"This way, Miss Vogel," Watson grumbled. "That's the car there. Bought it off your brother a few months ago."

He indicated a handsome Lincoln, a bit ordinary, but well maintained. It was not a very Vogel-ish sort of car.

My father had owned the very first automobile on the southern Oregon coast. He added car after car to our little garage, Loziers and Napiers and Stutzes, each one faster than the last. He never let anyone else drive his cars. He would crank up the motor and slip inside, giving us a nod before he pulled his driving goggles over his sea-gray eyes, and Frederick and I would whoop and holler like the foreman's children.

I couldn't imagine Frederick buying a car as prosaic as a Lincoln, let alone selling it off to a man like Ebenezer Watson. I hoped he'd found something with a bigger engine or better seats.

Watson opened the back door for me, and I slid inside. The interior gave off a strangely sweet smell, familiar and yet not.

"Next stop, Storm Break," Watson called out. I could see him watching me in the rearview mirror. I folded my hands and studied them where they lay in my lap. The gloves Christina had given me were supple, gray, the height of fashion.

My head inclined, I could just see a scrap of red out of the corner of my eye; I stooped to pick it up. It was a matchbook for The Singing Lotus Room, a Portland dance hall so known for its speakeasy only graft could explain the police department's blind eye. One of the other boarders at Mrs. Shavington's—a typist at The Oregonian—claimed the speakeasy was only the least tawdry of the dance hall's illegitimate activities.

"Do you smoke, Miss Vogel?"

He held out his hand for the matchbook. I hesitated a moment and then passed it to him. Did he really drink at that place?

Did he dance with the good time girls and buy opium from the Chinese gangsters working out of the basement? Or was he just a small-town foreman with big ideas for his vacations?

"It's a nice little place," he said, waving the matchbook in the rearview mirror. "The music's got nothing on the bands I've seen in San Francisco, though. Frisco's great. Your brother and I try to make it down every couple of months."

"I had no idea you two were so cosmopolitan."

He chuckled, and I had to turn my gaze away from him. That mustache. Those damp lips. I peered into the woods crowding against the road. How different they looked from the scraped and scoured forests around Portland! So dark, so lush, so filled with the promise of wild things.

My fingers tightened around each other. If anyone could see me, they would have only seen a young woman with fashionably short hair and good clothes, hands clasped properly across her knees. But inside my gloves, my fingers twisted and squeezed like beasts hungry for air.

TWO

AND THEN THERE they were: the gates of Storm Break, the
wrought iron fierce and black, the tops of its metal spokes
neatly spiked like shark fins. Someone had thrown them open for
us, and the car turned into the drive as if we were simply making
another left turn, the tires crunching on the crushed oyster shells
as if they were ordinary gravel.

I pressed the palm of my glove against the glass of the window
to pull it all in closer to me. How much it had changed in the
six years since I'd left. The maples overhung the drive now,
their limbs fat enough to dapple the ground below with shade.
The blacker spruce hung back, cautious of the motorcar and
its growling, stinking engine. False solomon's seal and trillium
glinted white beneath the dancing ferns.

The drive eased around a corner, slipped over the graceful
arc of the Storm Creek bridge, turned left again, and then the
house peeked out at us, a trillium itself, shy and glinting between
the trees. Only the third floor showed, and then it slipped away,
barred from view by the now-defensive spruce. Even over the
engine, I heard the lowing of cows.

"Your brother's farm has been doing well," Watson pronounced. "Four calves just this week."

"So it's making him money then?"

"Well." He paused. "It's not about money, per se. It's about changing the face of agriculture in Oregon. You know, your brother hopes to double the size of the herd this year. There's talk of starting a cheese factory soon."

I couldn't imagine my father showing interest in the birth of livestock or planning a factory for something as unprofitable as cheese. I certainly hoped the sawmill and the shipyards kept up with Frederick's experiments. New wives didn't come cheaply.

We both went silent, because now the trees cleared and the white flanks of the house appeared, achingly pale in the late spring sunshine. Here, nothing had changed. Perfect boxwood cubes still marked off every foot of the drive, their dimensions to my mother's exacting standards. The pair of palms she'd brought with her from San Francisco framed the front entrance, their massive blue and white china pots still shiny and unchipped. I half expected Maman to step out of the door to greet me.

"Look, there's the staff now," Watson noted.

The staff stood in the semi-circle of the carriage turnabout, blue uniforms crisp, aprons starched, caps on straight. Mrs. Franklin stood at attention beside the front door, Beamon and Monsieur Alain at her sides. Beside them stood a pimple-faced maid and a young man in gardening boots. Was this it? Could a house as grand as Storm Break run on a staff of only five? And if the staff knew I was arriving, why hadn't anyone brought my niece down to greet me?

The car stopped.

"I reckon you're home, Miss Vogel."

For a moment, I just sat there, straining my neck to peer up to the top of the house, taking in the white siding of the upper floors, the delicate casement windows. I'd grown used to fine houses, walking with my students in the finest of Portland's neighborhoods. But Storm Break did not present herself as a *house.* Its dormers looked down at the world with a presence no mere dwelling could ever convey. She was very much a lady, and we were there to serve her.

Beamon stepped forward and opened the car door.

"Miss Vogel. We are all very glad to see you." His voice sounded as mournful and British as ever, but I could see real feeling in his constrained smile.

"I'm very glad to be here, Mr. Beamon." I followed him toward the house.

I smiled from him to the maid and the boy, but the smile nearly escaped me when my eyes met Mrs. Franklin's. Her face stayed hard as stone, her mouth set in a stiff moue of disapproval. The sight of her made me keenly aware of my travel-disheveled clothing. Mrs. Franklin was the cleanest, tidiest being I had ever known.

She was trained to be, of course. Before my mother came to Oregon, Mrs. Franklin had been her maid. When my father told Maman he was having Storm Break built, she had sent Mrs. Franklin back to San Francisco to study with her own mother's housekeeper, so someone she trusted could run the house to her exacting standards. It must have worked. No one had ever run a house as thoroughly and carefully as Mrs. Franklin did.

"Good morning. Mrs. Franklin." I looked around again. Cleared my throat. "Do you know where my niece is?"

She inclined her head minutely. "Resting, Miss Vogel. I didn't think you would want me to bother her."

I drew myself to my full height, hoping it made me look a bit more kempt. "I see. Well, I'll check on her myself, I suppose. Could you see to my things, Mrs. Franklin? Beamon, if you could show me to my charge."

Mrs. Franklin glanced down at my wrinkled skirt and her lips tightened. I tried not to flinch away from her as I pushed through the front door.

It looked just the same: the entry's mirror-polished parquet floor in shades of oak and cherry. The great staircase, connecting the two wings and the two main floors. A rose-patterned runner warmed its treads, which rose to the landing where I had so often huddled with my sketchbook and my pastels, trying to capture the magnificence of the portrait hanging on the wall. The painting was easiest to see from the landing, especially if you came down the stairs that split off to the children's wing. In the morning I could get up, dash down to the landing and see the picture of my mother in her cotillion best, her blue dress a wonder of layers and lace. It was like the sea, that dress, all froth and foam on the surface, mystery at its depths.

I couldn't help but turn myself so I could greet that image before I took in anything else inside the house. My mother looked down at me, fresh and young and somehow still all-knowing, her eyes unreadable as they stared down at me.

For a second I lost my bearings; the parquet floor seemed to give a wriggle like a dog pressing itself against the hand of a beloved but long absent master—a notion I thought ridiculous at the time. But looking back, dear Lillian, I think it's where the nightmare really began.

I stumbled a little.

"Miss?"

"It's nothing, Beamon. The sea journey."

The butler inclined his head gravely. "This way, Miss." Beamon directed me past the staircase and into the lower hallway. Not up the stairs, but toward the kitchen.

"Where are you taking me? Where is my niece?"

He looked back at me, the mild expression on his face as close to a shout of surprise as he ever managed. "To Miss Abigail's room. As you requested."

"Shouldn't she be in one of the children's rooms?"

We passed the kitchen door and turned a corner. The hardwood changed to drab linoleum. I had almost never been this far back in the house. This was Mrs. Franklin's territory.

He opened the door to the back stairs. "Her nanny preferred to have her nearby."

"That woman was fired over a year ago."

There was no runner, patterned or not, to quiet the thuds of our feet here in the stairwell. The walls leaned in nearly to the points of my elbows.

"Mr. Vogel gave no orders to have her moved."

We passed the second floor doorway, which only the servants used, and continued up. He opened the door at the top of the stairs. A gray ribbon of light lit up his face. The overhang of Storm Break's roof kept most of the sunshine out of this hallway, the servants' quarters.

The air smelled of strong lye soap and beeswax. At least someone had the presence of mind to whitewash the walls, which gave a bit of brightness to the space. Spartan it was, but it was still nicer than the quarters I'd kept when I first left Storm Break to work as a teacher.

Beamon nodded at the green door here at the end of the corridor. "This is the little lady's."

I laid my hand on the knob, thought again, and rapped gently. "Abigail? It's me, your aunt June."

Silence.

"May I come in?"

A faint rustling answered. I steeled myself and opened the door.

The little figure on the bed sat outlined in muslin patches, a quilted ghost surrounded by sticks and rocks. A book and an unshaped clump of brown fur sat on the pillow beside it.

"Abigail?"

With a soft shushing, the book slid down the curve of the pillow, balanced a brief second on the edge of the bed, and fell to the floor with a crash. The fur thing went, too.

The quilt whipped back from the girl's face and she flew up at me.

"Why'd you do that?"

Her tiny fists battered my chest, her face one red raw expanse of open mouth. I took an inadvertent step backward.

She flung herself to the floor. "Book, oh, book. Are you all right?"

She whipped the fur bundle to her chest. "And Pewter, too! Oh, Pewter, are you all right?"

White skirt or not, I knelt beside the creature. My brother had never sent me a photograph of his daughter, and now I could see why. She wasn't ugly, not quite, but she lacked any resemblance to her parents. Nature had stolen away from her my brother's pink cheeks and fine fox-like eyes, Blanche's curling black mane and full rosy lips. The pointed chin and pinched features of this creature, made of the drabbest of colors, had nothing to recommend them to a family of certain beauties. I could understand too well.

"Are your friends all right, Abigail?"

Her lower lip pushed itself forward. "I'm not talking to you."

"Do you know who I am?"

"You're my new nanny." She twisted her neck so her anger-slitted eyes could glint at me. "I have promised to hate you."

"I am not your nanny. I am your aunt, here to get to know you as a special treat." In this circumstance, the carefully prepared words felt implausible, but I pushed on. "Why have you decided to hate me?"

The girl turned the fur bundle so its pointed muzzle and green button eyes could look out at me. I'd had dolls as a little girl, and my father had once brought me a mohair rabbit from San Francisco, but this animal being, whatever it was, had obviously been hand-sewn from a scrap of some abandoned old fur. Its form conveyed no softness, no friendly loving face to invite a child into companionable imagination. This thing was as stiff and cold as Abigail herself.

"You're an interloper." Abigail used her hand to make the animal's head bob up and down as she spoke the words in a different voice, ancient and weather-rasped. "You've come to ruin everything."

I stood up. My feet and ankles tingled with pins and needles, and the rest of me was no more steady.

"I'll see you at dinner tonight, Abigail. Until then, you can stay in your room and reconsider the way you treat your family."

Her head shot forward like a snake's. "It's not even lunch yet!"

"Perhaps you should have thought of that before you let your friend say something so cruel."

I turned on my heel and strode to the door. I could feel Abigail making hideous faces at my back, but I did not turn around. Only when the door had closed behind me did I pause. I heard rustling again, books and sticks and the muslin scrap quilt being rearranged.

"She's going to regret treating us like this, Pewter," she said, very clearly. "We're going to make her pay."

There was no one in the servants' hallway to see me hug my arms around myself as I retreated back down the stairs.

THREE

BUT MY PLACE was the only one set when I went to the dining room. After the words I'd exchanged with Abigail, it was almost a relief. The maid managed to stammer out an excuse of tiredness for my charge; Mrs. Franklin did not show herself in the hall or in the butlery, but I could feel her eyes on me. Waiting to see if I would act like my mother—to claim my authority and demand my niece obey my wishes. But years in the classroom had taught me I had little interest in demanding obedience from anyone.

I quickly ate my well-prepared meal—Monsieur Alain still worked magic in the kitchen—and went upstairs. I couldn't help but feel that if I spun around, I would find Mrs. Franklin just behind me, waiting for me to dirty something.

My shoulders square, my posture straight, I closed my bedroom door on the long, watchful hallway and sank onto my bed. This. This was why I had resisted all of Frederick's invitations for Christmas and summer vacations. The staff, always watching me, as if they were the eyes of the very house. Waiting for me to slip up, to show them I had no more right to their service than the lowest footman. To expose the common, ordinary nature of my mind and body.

My mother and Blanche had never feared such discovery. Both born in San Francisco from the same moneyed lineage, something inside them allowed them to behave like Continental aristocrats. It couldn't have been mere riches that allowed them such grace. Perhaps it was beauty: the beauty they held, the beauty that had always surrounded them. To be mousy-haired and stocky and freckled had somehow glassed off beauty and poise from my world. No matter how polished or gleaming the surfaces around me, I left fingerprints.

And cracked, pitted fingerprints at that. I peeled off my new gray gloves, wincing a little. My right index fingertip had split open sometime during dinner. Not enough to bleed—only enough to sting, to bite, to irritate. For me, our condition—"ichthyosis," the doctors had called it, when my mother took first Frederick and then me to visit them—was an endless irritation. Cheap soaps or scalding water meant my fingers cracked and peeled. Cold weather called for tubs of hand cream and the sleekest, softest of gloves.

But at least for me, it was only an irritation. Boys get much more of the "ichthys" effect. "Ichthys" from the Greek for "fish." Poor Frederick.

It had been a constant irritation to Maman that her children didn't do a better job managing our coarse and sometimes scaly hides. She bought us vats of lotion, tubs of tar soap, and pair and after pair of gloves.

The funny thing is that my skin got better after I left Storm Break. All that washing and scrubbing and ointmenting, and what my flesh preferred was simply to be left alone. Only my hands, my hard-working, painting hands bothered me now.

I got up and circled through the room, searching for hand cream. At least my things had been tidied away with some care. The nervous little maid, I supposed. Mrs. Franklin would never stoop to such an endeavor.

I found my cream on the vanity and began working its thick lavender scent into my fingers. Its smell reminded me of Mary, the silent, ink-stained writer whose rooms lay across the hallway from mine at the boarding house. If I closed my eyes, I would see her, all smoldering stares and black fingertips and unsmiling mouth. A mouth so full and delectable—I turned on heel and forced myself to focus on my old room.

Little had been changed in it. My mother had decorated the space before I left the nursery, and neither Blanche nor Frederick had taken notice of its furnishings. The pieces looked outdated these days, with their cabriole legs and cherry varnishes, the formal shapes and colors my mother preferred. No dolls, of course. Maman had thrown all of them away that horrible day.

I went to my bookshelf, its childish volumes about animals and history the sole friends I'd had before I was allowed into the library downstairs. The bottom shelf remained devoted to my sketchbooks. I stooped to brush my fingertip over their spines, still neatly filed by date. My fingertip paused. There. A gap where there shouldn't be. Someone had taken one of the notebooks.

Blanche, I was sure. The last few notebooks had contained so many sketches of her. No matter how little she liked me, her vanity would have driven her to want those pictures. And no one else would have felt so entitled to my things.

The clock on the staircase called out seven. Too early for even dinner when Maman was alive, let alone an hour for me to retreat to my room. Somehow I felt far more exhausted than I had ever felt after a day's work at the preparatory academy.

But at least this wretched house had the cure for the ache in my back and the stiffness in my neck! My father had loved his gadgets, and Storm Break's plumbing was a miracle of hot water and ceramic luxury. Before I'd left home, I used to envy my parents their great marble bathroom with its series of spigots and handles and copper pipes. Now I understood that even the small tiled bathroom of the children's wing was a wonder. At the boarding house, I shared one tub and a very small hot water boiler with six other women. It had been years since I'd gotten to soak in a tub.

I found the towels the maid had left for me and stepped out into the hallway. I hesitated a moment, certain someone had just passed by my door. I could still feel their eyes on me.

Except that I was alone. Only the door to Frederick's old bedroom stood open, the space beyond as impersonal as a dormitory. A faint stink of camphor and tar ointment still wafted out, the ghost of our childhoods. I closed the bathroom door against it, but the scent remained, clinging to me or perhaps merely seeping from my disquieted memories.

I found the hook for the towel and hung it up beside the tub. And stopped. Someone had left a clothes brush beside the ceramic soap rest.

Right there, its tortoiseshell handle on top of the delicate pink cake of soap.

My hand trembled as I reached out for the brush. Maman's initials still glinted in gold script on the back, as fresh as it had looked when I was a child. How could its horsehair bristles still be so clean? How could they be the pale color of oats and not stained from night after night of scouring our flesh?

An image of Maman flashed through my head, leaning over me and my dolls, her body quaking with rage, the brush in her hand, the brush—

But no. That was years ago. I held the brush tight so my hand would stop trembling. I went to the window and threw it open.

And yes, dear Lillian, flung the brush into the bushes.

I spun toward the door. I would fill the air with my own scents, my lavender lotion, my geranium soap, my sweetly perfumed talc. That I could do. I couldn't turn off my memories, not with them glinting out of every surface, but I could shroud them in perfume and beauty. I could cover my hands in balm and forget the nights Maman would scour me—forget even the day Maman had forced me to scrub the tiles in this bathroom like one of the maids, scrub them until my skin burned red and cracked and she filled the bleeding seams with camphor and tar.

You don't like dirt so much now, do you? she hissed in my memory.

"Shut up, Maman," I snarled, and grabbed the door handle.

The window I'd just opened slammed shut, the glass vibrating in the frame.

It was nothing, of course. A faulty mechanism. A breeze. I turned my attention back to the door knob and twisted it hard. The porcelain spun in my palm, but the door did not open.

I shook the knob. Nothing.

The bathtub behind me gave a sudden shriek, followed by the drum of water against cast iron. I spun to face it. The taps spewed water at full force.

I ran to turn them off. I hadn't touched them; I couldn't understand how they had spun themselves open. I clawed at the slippery x-shaped handles. They refused to turn. Hot water scalded my arm.

"Damn it!"

I put my weight into the taps. Steam rose from the bottom of the tub, twining around my face and hair and reeking of tar. I coughed as I drew in a lungful of the stuff.

"Help," I gasped. It wasn't much of a shout. The tub vibrated against my body, the power of the water shaking its sides. The pipes groaned and grumbled.

"Help!"

The cast iron shuddered as if an engine deep within it had gone into higher gear. I pounded the taps with my palm. How could they stick like this? I gripped them harder and twisted with all my strength.

The door crashed open, and the bathtub gave a lurch. The pipes shrieked louder.

"Stop it," a girl's voice ordered. "Stop it right now!"

With an agonized screech, the taps spun in my hand. For a second, my fingers refused to release the handles, and then I fell back, clutching my reddened hands to my chest.

I kicked myself away from the tub until my back rested against the far wall. The tub sat quietly, ordinarily, only a fine veil of steam twisting above its horrible taps. I risked a glance at the doorway.

Abigail stood there panting, staring at the tub. She looked paler than ever, and her teeth, yellow and square, showed in her gasping mouth.

"Abigail? Are you all right?"

She turned her gaze toward me as if she had only just remembered I was there. "You must really be my aunt if the house wants to kill you, too."

Without another word, she spun around and vanished down the hall. I should have chased after her, I suppose, but it took me a long, long time to make my legs support me and to wobble out to my bedroom.

I STRUGGLED TO fall asleep that night, Lillian. How could I sleep? Every time I closed my eyes the scene repeated itself. Were my hands too slippery with balm? Was the old boiler so long unused it had choked itself with rust that gurgled and screamed inside the bathroom pipes? Had Abigail been standing outside, holding the door shut the whole time? But how could a slight little girl be that strong?

And the watching. The watching. I couldn't help but feel it even as I lay in my own room, the door locked against intruders. Cruel eyes still watched me and reveled in my insomnia.

I turned on my lamp and sat up in bed, hugging the blankets to my chest. A tiny, hysterical bubble of laughter rose up in my chest. I'd sworn in my mother's house. The words "damn it" had come out of my perfect, pure Vogel mouth. Oh, if Maman could know what else that mouth has done, what she would have said! I could imagine the paint peeling off her very portrait.

Out in the hallway, a door slammed shut. I slid down in my bed. It had been the bathroom door. I was sure of that. Abigail?

It banged open.

I turned out my light and pulled the covers over my head. A few moments later the door slammed again. The girl was trying to unnerve me. I laid there and waited for it to thump once more, but I fell into an exhausted sleep before it repeated itself.

FOUR

I WOKE AT my usual time, unrested and certain I needed to
ask Abigail what she had meant about the house. It took me
the better part of the next day to track her down. She moved
somehow invisibly; I might round a corner in any room, sure I
saw a flash of wild brown hair, and find the maid watching me
with big, uneasy eyes, but Maureen—that was her big, confident
name, poor girl—hadn't caught even a glimpse of my niece.
Monsieur Alain had noticed a few rolls gone missing from the
pantry, but could not remember the last time he actually laid
eyes on the child of the house. Beamon seemed surprised I was
even looking for her. Mrs. Franklin, of course, was too busy
with her own duties to notice anything like a child, and looked
offended I'd even asked.

As I expanded my search to the grounds, the signs appeared.
At first I thought them inadvertent clues, the raisin cookie
accidently dropped on the back stairs, one of my own books
forgotten on a stump. I knew I had misjudged her when I found
the ploughman's lunch set in a lovely clearing, a sun-dappled space
hidden behind one of my brother's barns. I realized, nibbling one
of Monsieur's magnificent pickles, that Abigail had her own plans
for me, and that if she watched from the bushes, she did not wish
to be seen. I bundled the empty crocks and plate into the picnic

blanket and slung it over my arm. I could see a pattern of broken ferns that suggested a secret pathway to the beach.

I followed such tiny hints and gestures all around my brother's property. It felt like a gift. Most of the spaces she arranged for me to see hadn't existed when I had been a child; the forests around Storm Break had been cleared for the lumber that shaped the house's halls, leaving only a scrim of trees for privacy. Outside of my mother's gardens, only mud and broken tree limbs had lain, uninhabitable and uninviting. The beauty of these woods was nothing I had ever known.

I couldn't help thanking Abigail even as my legs complained. How wonderfully free it felt to spend all day under the trees and looking at flowers! My eyes felt more alive searching the ground for her tiny footprints than they had ever been sketching portraits for Portland's high society.

Then I crested the hill and heard the growl and shriek of the Vogel Sawmill, and I realized she had brought me to the final edge of our family's land. I followed her path down the hill's flank, catching glimpses of log trucks on the road below. If I had taken the road, I would have come to the mill in less than three miles—maybe an hour's walk if the mud wasn't too bad. I would have seen nothing but log trucks and the occasional car.

I came out on the verge behind the mill, a bushy green expanse occasionally used to stockpile logs but currently empty. Heaps of woody debris marked off the areas when the trucks loaded and unloaded, a sort of prickly scarf encircling the mill's cluster of buildings.

The best parts of my childhood had happened right here, not so much in the cavernous, screaming space of the main sawmill, but mostly inside the little white office where my father and his assistants ran the operation. The constant roar and vibration of the machines kept me company as I sat on the rug before the little wood stove, sketching on scraps of paper the accountant gave me. A part of me wanted to climb the short set of stairs to see if there were still peppermint discs in the jar on top of the filing cabinet.

Then I caught a glimpse of Abigail crouched beside the nearest heap of smashed tree branches, beckoning for me to join her.

"Shush," she whispered before I even said a word. She pointed toward the log truck idling beside the office.

Three men stood beside it, and one of them I knew: Ebenezer Watson. I could not hear his voice over the truck and the saws, but I could see his ugly mouth flapping. Another man waved his hands as he shouted nonsense sounds at Watson. The third, slender and dressed in carefully patched overalls , his head bowed as if to let the noise flow over it. My mouth fell open a little when I caught a glimpse of his face beneath his straw hat and realized he was colored.

Abigail's slender fingers folded around mine. I wondered if she had ever seen a colored man before. I wondered if her father, like mine, kept a white hood and robe in the back of his closet. I very much hoped not.

Watson slapped the back of the truck driver's head, sending his straw hat to the ground. Abigail squeezed my hand harder, or maybe I squeezed hers.

Shaking his head, Watson headed toward the office, his friend behind him. The colored man stooped to pick up his hat and got into the truck. Watson paused on the stairs to pull out a cigarette case. His friend proffered a matchbook from his pocket.

"I hate him," she breathed. "Every time he comes to see Papa, he pinches my cheek." She made a tiny sound, like a stifled growl. The matchbook made a soft whoosh as every match suddenly blazed to life.

"Shit!" Watson yelped.

I clapped my hand over my smile.

He dropped the flaming matchbook and stamped it out, his boots shaking the flimsy risers so hard we could see them where we stood. His head swiveled to see if anyone else had seen. I dove back behind the pile of broken branches and sawdust. Despite me tugging on her arm, Abigail watched another second and then crawled back into hiding, her shoulders shaking with silent laughter. She turned to face me, beaming, her eyes bright.

A stray spark could have lit those matches. There was no reason to connect her angry words to the ball of fire in Watson's hand. But I couldn't help remembering the tremendous crash when the door opened yesterday, the door I could not open with all my adult strength. I couldn't help seeing the light shining in those brown eyes not as just laughter but pride.

The smile folded itself back inside her sharp face.

"Now you know I can do things, Aunt June."

She reached out her hand to me, and I tried not to let my hesitation show when I took it. But Lillian, my mind was uneasy as we made our way back through the woods.

AFTER OUR AFTERNOON at the mill, we each went our separate ways as if nothing had happened. But after a rushed and anxious nightly toilette—although I had found a way to prop the bathroom door open—I returned to my room and found Abigail had dragged her ratty quilt into the far corner of my room and curled up on it. I confess my first urge when I saw her, clutching Pewter's ragged shape to her cheek, was to wake her and send her back to her room. I even stooped over her a minute, ready to shake her shoulder.

But then I remembered the bright, startling flare of that matchbook. I remembered how scared I had been, seeing pride light up her expression. There was none of that on her face now. She looked as small and helpless as any child I'd ever seen. A set of freckles made a perfect triangle on the tip of her nose.

I pulled the blanket up to her chin and turned out the light. I didn't sleep much or sleep well, but I wouldn't have anyway.

FIVE

WE SPENT THE next few weeks inseparable, Abigail, Pewter, and I. I watched her with uncertainty. She happily showed me all the paths she liked to haunt in the forest. I sketched her and surreptitiously watched her as she drew oddly shaped animals with my pastels. She held my hand and introduced me to every cow in my brother's barn.

Did I fear her, Lillian? Knowing what she could do? Of course I did. But the more time we spent outside of Storm Break, the easier it was to forget that she might be anything but a normal little girl. A neglected, ferociously curious, and wildly, passionately clever little girl, but a little girl nonetheless.

And we were surprisingly happy, the two of us. Outside, it was easy to enjoy Abigail's company. She rarely *did things*, as she had put it that day at the sawmill. Once she tripped over a sand pail we had carelessly left on the path, and I saw it fly a hundred yards up the hill. I pretended she kicked it.

I was good at pretending I didn't see things. I was good at closing my eyes and telling myself they had tricked me. But outside of Storm Break, I didn't usually need to.

Since we had no obligations except to stay out from underfoot, we found every excuse to get out of the house. We ate what we liked and went where we pleased. In the sunset cove beneath the cliffs, we waded in the sea and gathered shells (although Pewter took to sunbathing after one too many tumbles into the pitted pools where the sea flowers bloomed). We walked to Yarrow. We stayed outside as long as we could, longer and longer every day.

Abigail seemed to thrive. Under the summer sun, her cheeks grew pink and brown-dappled, and her hair streaked itself gold. Even my skin improved out there, the dry places scrubbed smooth by sand and salt, the sea breeze softened even the deepest cracks.

I knew our peace and sunshine couldn't last. Inside Storm Break's walls, I still felt something watching us intently. Even at night, when the staff had gone to bed.

I didn't sleep much. I lay in bed and listened for something I wasn't sure I could name. I lay in bed, Lillian, and I waited for disaster to strike down my quiet happiness.

THE DAY MY brother's new wife arrived at Storm Break was one of those golden days Abigail and I walked down to the town of Yarrow to dawdle in front of the one mercantile and buy treats at Anderson's bakery. The baker and his wife were among those rare people Abigail liked and who liked her back. She admired their strength, I think, the way they could both carry the massive trays of bread and biscuits, each metal sheet longer than their young son Teddy stood high. She admired, too, the wondrous way the baker could flick the silver shaker of dusting sugar, transforming anything, even a simple square of gingerbread, into a snowy field. There was so much magic in that bakery.

What must it have been like, growing up in a family so sweet and good, and not one that waited and watched for you to make the slightest mistake? I couldn't help thinking that, no more than I could help fearing, for a horrible second, that my mother would punish me for spilling powdered sugar on my blouse front. *You're so filthy*, she would have said. *No child of mine should be such a mess.*

But I let Abigail be just as much a mess as she wished to be,
and we walked home stuffing ourselves on treats, our shoes hung
over our shoulders by their laces, the buttons on our collars
undone. For June, the sun already seared with August's heat.

A car passed us, a fine car the color of cordovan leather, and in
the passenger seat, a young woman with big eyes pressed her palm
against the window—just as I had—as if she could push her way
out into our freedom. I smiled after her, polishing the last speck of
gingerbread off my finger with the red-hot tip of my tongue.

Then Abigail choked on the end of her cake and spat it out.
"That's Papa's car!" She burst into a run, and I ran after her.

WHEN WE BURST through the front door, my brother stood on the
landing of the great staircase, his hand on the small of his bride's
back, pointing out some detail on the portrait of my mother
hanging above them. Maman's eyes stared down at us all, fresh
as ice, blue as jellyfish, hard as the basalt bones of the world. The
slim, slight girl in the curve of my brother's arms took the full
weight of those eyes and didn't even let her shoulders bow.

At the sight of her, I realized what I had felt for my
boardinghouse poet was nothing but a minor dalliance. My
brother's new wife stole the breath from my lungs. The rich honey-
gold of her hair, the color of late afternoon sunshine itself, had been
rolled into glossy twists at once complementing and undercutting
the modern lines of her walking suit. Peering attentively into the
painting, my brother's bride looked like nothing so much as a
modern Guinevere, her chin and long white brow possessed of a
medieval purity.

"June!" Frederick surged down the stairs, arms outstretched.
I found myself enveloped in the scents of tobacco smoke and
woodruff, hair pomade and luxurious cologne. He smelled as
if he had truly become the lord and overseer of Storm Break, a
man of riches and the world. He smelled like my father.

He pulled back to look me over, and I studied him in return.
I saw now lines around his eyes that hadn't been there on his
last trip to Portland. The curl in his russet hair looked just as

delightful as when I'd seen him last, the thin line of his mustache just as suggestive of Hollywood glamor, the cut of his jacket slim as ever, but his face gave away something crueler than the mere march of time.

"How long has it been, Sis? Two years?"

Although he hadn't yet greeted Abigail, he stooped and hoisted her into his arms. Most girls of nine would not suffer such indignity, but she burrowed into his neck with relish.

"Two at Christmas, I think." The muscles in my cheeks hurt, my smile stretched them so much. "I've missed you, Frederick." I hadn't realized how much until this very moment.

"Is this your sweet baby sister, Freddie?"

Frederick beamed and pulled his wife into his side. "Oh, dear heart, yes. June, this is my Lillian, heart of my heart, light of my life. I was introduced to her by one of our partners in San Francisco."

She put out her hand—*you*, Lillian, *you* put out your little white hand—and I shook it, not knowing what I shook into my life. You couldn't have known either, no matter what you say now.

"Why, you're barely older than I am, June." Your voice was as honeyed as your hair.

And "barely older" was something of a stretch. You still haven't told me your age, but at the time I guessed you no more than twenty, if that. The suppleness of your skin suggested you had never set foot out of doors, and from the magnificent creaminess of your forehead and cheeks I was certain you had never once gotten an acne spot.

Abigail made a sound that might have been a hiss, but with her face buried in Frederick's shoulder, it was hard to tell.

"It's lovely to meet you, Lillian." I freed my hand from her very warm one and tucked a strand of hair behind my ear. I was keenly aware that I had left my bobby pins on my bedside stand that morning, and that there was moss caught in the seams of my brogues. "But what are you two doing here? I thought you had nearly another month in Mexico."

Lillian pulled a face. Frederick chuckled. "My dear found the heat disagreed with her."

"Too many Hollywood types, too many parties," she disagreed. "Besides, the climate was simply too dry. I need the fog like I need air!"

I couldn't help smiling back at her. "You'll get plenty of that here at Storm Break."

Her eyes wandered over the white walls and heavy beams of the entrance hall. "That will suit me."

Abigail wiggled free of Frederick's grasp and moved to my side, her eyes fixed on her new stepmother's face. I had a feeling she would take her time deciding if this new member of the family would suit her.

SIX

S O THAT IS how we met: You, my brother's bride, and me, my niece's keeper. You, the consummate beauty; me, stout and plain, and neither of us quite what we seemed. I feel so guilty remembering the way things unfolded for us in that house. I was a terrible sister, wasn't I? And yet despite those pricklings of conscience, I take such pleasure in remembering that first day and what it was to see you with eyes that had never filled themselves with such a wonder as your face.

On that night, I crept out of my room after Abigail had fallen asleep, envying her that freedom. I didn't want to think about my brother's wife with her polished gold hair, but her face kept floating behind my eyelids, all curved chin and broad smile, her lips very pink and her teeth strangely small.

At this end of the hallway, the soft lights of the downstairs lamps failed to penetrate the muzzy darkness. The bathroom—a block of wood nailed into the frame to keep it from a repeat of its performance on my first night in the house—lay to my left, invisible. A faucet gave the occasional *plip* of escaping water.

A soft thumping to my right made me pause in the dark. The skin between my shoulder blades tingled as if someone's gaze rested there.

The thumping repeated itself, a basso counterpoint to the dripping faucet. The sound came from beyond the sweep of the staircase, from the hallway unfurling out of the stairs' right arm, the hallway where my parents had once slept and now my brother and his Lillian claimed for their own.

But I realized just then that I was not the only one sleepless that night: a figure in white slipped out of one of the bedrooms. My brother's new wife—you, Lilian, but I must steel myself and put this space between us so I can finish this story—leaned back, putting all her slight weight into the recalcitrant door.

I hurried toward her. "What's the matter?"

She startled hard enough to lose her grip on the doorknob and then nearly her balance. I caught her by the elbow. She wore an old-fashioned one-piece union suit, so at odds to the glamorous ensemble she'd worn this afternoon I nearly laughed.

She pulled her arm free and wrapped it around her torso. "Don't tell Frederick you saw me like this."

I could only look at her, perplexed.

"It's unladylike, isn't it?" she whispered.

And in workingmen's long underwear, her hair snugly braided, she did look more like a boy than the fine lady I'd met downstairs. A young boy, at that.

I made an X over my breast just the way I'd seen the girls at the school. "Cross my heart."

The door gave a quiet thump.

"It won't stop doing that. I was almost asleep, and it just started banging for no reason."

I twisted the knob, which turned smoothly and firmly just as it ought, and then opened the door to inspect the hinges. The bedside lamp lit the room amber, leaving shadows thick-piled in the corners. Whatever poise I'd felt standing in the hallway seeped out of my skin.

After my mother died, Blanche had spent months redoing this room, replacing all of Maman's blue brocades and dark woods with roses and cream, as light and feminine as Blanche's French perfume. But the old things must have simply gone into the attic. On the mantle stood Maman's Chinese ginger jar, and her bronze dragon-dogs framed the fireplace. Lillian's two trunks sat at the foot of the bed, one open and still packed tight.

That wretched Mrs. Franklin.

Of course this was Mrs. Franklin's doing. Who else would have turned this place into a shrine to my mother? Who else would have ordered Maureen to leave those trunks unpacked?

The door thumped behind us, a deeper, louder bang.

"I'll see you unpacked tomorrow, Lillian. That should have been done for you."

She stepped between me and the trunks. "Oh, it's all right. I'm used to doing for myself. We didn't have any servants at our house." Her eyebrows drew together. "Don't tell Frederick that either, please."

Standing in that half-light, her feathers still packed, Lillian revealed herself—inadvertently, I'm sure—as a creature far tougher and wilder than the sweet canary I had taken her for. She gilded herself in secrets and hid her claws beneath their pretty shimmer. Well, if I had been pretty, perhaps I would have done the same thing.

The door thumped, then again, and again. It was picking up speed.

I snatched up her pillow and stuffed it in the door crack. The door flew open, smashing against the wall and then ricocheting back into the pillow. A little rain of dust, oddly golden, sprinkled down on the pillowcase.

Lillian grabbed my hand.

"Let's put you in a guest room tonight."

I had to struggle to get the door open, especially one-handed. She kept a fast grip on my left hand as I led her down the hall to the room at the head of the staircase. It smelled musty and the pillows had gone flat with inattention, but the door remained closed when we shut it behind us.

I opened the window and let a whisper of the sea inside. "You ought to sleep all right here."

She scrambled into bed, burrowing her feet beneath the covers as if she was somehow cold on this pleasant summer's night. "Are you sure?"

Did I tell the truth? Did I tell her I had no idea if any part of this house—whether bedroom, bathtub, or stepdaughter—would ever accept her or let her relax? That it seemed to be growing noisier and more watchful every night?

"I hope." I crossed to the door and paused. "And if you don't, I'm just down the hall. By the bathroom." I opened the door. "Maybe don't wash up by yourself, though."

She opened her mouth and then closed it. She pulled the comforter up to her shoulders. "You can tell me about that when the sun is up."

I gave a little laugh. Then I made my way through the dark, finished my business in the bathroom, and found Abigail sitting on my bed, Pewter clutched to her chest.

"Who were you talking to?"

I slipped into the bed as if I didn't mind the look on her face. "Lillian. Her door wouldn't shut properly."

"The house doesn't like her very much, does it?"

She smiled an ugly smile. For the first time in weeks, I wondered if it was she that shut me in the bathroom that night. I pushed the thought away.

"Let's get some sleep, Abigail. I'm tired."

She turned off the bedside lamp. In a few minutes her nose began its telltale squeaking. I lay there listening to it a long time, hoping a door would thump in the hallway.

Soft ragtime music and morning sunshine spilled out the opening between door and frame, but I rapped on the study door with an engrained sense of awe. This was the one room denied to me in my childhood years, its heavy mahogany door sealing off the mystery of my father's life. On those rare occasions he wasn't traveling to San Francisco or Seattle or our shipyards in Grays Harbor, he would shut himself up in his study for hours at a time, and I would sit outside the door with my pencils and sketchbooks, listening for some tiny sound that would explain what he did when he was out of sight.

I couldn't say my father and I were close, or that he understood me more than my mother did. He simply didn't loathe me the way she did. We spent less and less time together as I grew older. The week before he died we had spent the most time together we had in years. He'd broken his ankle on the way to one of his nighttime meetings. Blanche insisted on bringing him meals, but I was the one who sat with him and read to him and brought him his medicine and brandy. And then I came up the stairs with my tray and saw Blanche standing by his chair, wringing her white-gloved hands—she always wore gloves, and they were always white, spotless and white—and staring down at him with her face gone flat and pale. I knew without asking that he was gone.

I didn't feel empty until the day after his funeral. That's when I opened the door and sat down at his desk, sure this place, his sanctuary, would still retain something of him even if he was gone. It smelled like him, of sweet cherry pipe tobacco and cedar chips. But for all the ledgers stacked on the desk and the books surrounding it, I could get no sense of the man, his thoughts, his dreams.

In the bottom right desk drawer I found a bottle of bourbon and three daguerreotypes of naked women. I'd kept the lot of it.

I knocked on the door again to push away such thoughts.

The gramophone gave a burst of tinned ragtime and then cut out. "Come in."

I pushed open the door, and Frederick jumped to his feet. "June, come, come."

He pressed me in a hug and then sat back in his desk chair. He had replaced Father's with a newer version, the same color. The books filling the case behind the desk looked different, too. I remembered to take a seat.

"It's wonderful to see you so happy, Frederick."

"It's all credit to Lillian. She's so lively and kind, June-a-moon. I thought I loved Blanche, and of course I did, but I was so young. And Maman was so sure..." His cheeks went red, as he realized he had perhaps shared too much. "Anyway, Lillian is simply wonderful."

How much had Maman pressured him into marrying her precious cousin? I felt a wave of fury for her meddling, a fury so hot it took me by surprise. I had to clear my throat to compose myself. "How did you two meet?"

"Oh, one of my business contacts took me to a party at h
er mother's house. Such a remarkable woman, Mrs. Renault.

The widow of a shipbuilder, I believe. Somehow she rallied her spirits after his untimely demise to become one of San Francisco's leading lights. Her parties are attended by all of the most important businessmen."

"I hope their wives provide her some entertainment."

He frowned. "No, there are almost never women in attendance. But Mrs. Renault is one of those rare women who truly understands and appreciates the world of men."

I shifted in my seat, unwilling to point out the oddity of these parties. The hierarchy and structure of San Francisco's high society demanded adherence to a strict set of rules, and I knew my mother and Blanche—born and bred to serve as leading lights in that refined world—would have certainly snubbed any woman who behaved the way Frederick described Mrs. Renault.

"Did Lillian enjoy these gatherings as well?"

"Oh, yes! She was quite the belle of the ball. She knew everyone's name and their favorite drink and the whole crew admired her to no end. I think the reason so few of them made it to our wedding was pure jealousy!" He chuckled cheerfully.

I had my doubts about such a claim. But I smiled as if I agreed with him. "Perhaps you should throw a party here at Storm Break. A young woman deserves a big wedding celebration."

He clapped his hands. "Of course! And you can help Lillian plan the whole thing."

"What?" I could only stare at him. "Frederick, now that you and Lillian are home, I assumed you'd send me back to Portland. There's still enough time left in the season that I could secure a few portrait commissions."

He took my hands in his own. I could feel the rasp of his cracked fingers against my own dry skin. "Oh, no. You can't leave us so soon. Abigail adores you, and Lillian is dying to get to know you. She never had a sister, you know. You could teach her so much about family."

I pulled my hands free and patted his wrists gently. His cuffs had risen up, revealing a line of ashy scales where the dryness had taken hold. "I really need those commissions. My salary at the prep school—"

"You can paint Lillian!"

"What?" Once again, the conversation had twisted out of my expectations.

"She hates that picture of Maman on the landing. It's so old-fashioned, the colors so dull. You could create something more appropriate for the spirit of the house. And I'm sure I'd pay better than your average Portland doctor or lawyer."

In the wall beside me, a pipe gurgled noisily. Looking back, I remember that distinctly: that the house tried to warn me away.

But oh! to paint Lillian. That was all I could think of, dear one: what it would be like to paint your hair and those upturned eyes and that mouth which made all other mouths look insufficient for smiling.

"Yes," I said. "Yes." I said: "Yes."

SEVEN

MAUREEN HELPED ME bring my painting materials—brought from home with only the vaguest hopes of some landscape studies—out to the garden, Frederick's choice for the portrait's background. Abigail crept behind us, stopping to whisper to Pewter whenever I tried to catch her attention. I could feel her eyes on my neck the minute I turned around.

Maureen skidded on the brick steps, but I caught her elbow before she fell. "Are you all right?"

She dropped the newly stretched canvas on an azalea, and seeing my horrified expression, quickly balanced it on her foot. "I can't see nothing with this thing in my way."

"I can take it if you like. This crate is heavy, but it's not as unwieldy." I held out the wood box.

"Thanks."

There was an awkward moment as she nearly put her arm through the canvas and the crate tried to wriggle out of my hands. I managed not to break anything and got the canvas tucked under my arm.

Maureen shifted the crate to rest against her torso. "You're not half-bad, Miss Vogel. Folks said you were the weird one, but I reckon that's just idle talk."

"Oh. I…" I couldn't imagine myself the topic of any "folks'" conversation. "Thank you."

"There's always talk about the house in town. Even when it was just Mr. Vogel, people told stories about the bunch of yous. Your ma with her parties. You, quiet as a clam. Mrs. Blanche with her bad end, of course. I'm surprised folks say the place is cursed!"

I blinked at her impudence, but she was already trudging down the steps toward the heart of the garden. I could only shake my head.

But the glory of the garden and the fine day swept away the maid's odd words. The breeze off the sea softened the sun's heat. I had never known such a stretch of good weather at Storm Break. It cast the garden in gold and alabaster, the marble fountain in the central courtyard nearly glowing. I squeezed my eyes shut, my heart suddenly aching.

Did I believe there were ghosts in the house? I knew, didn't I, that my father hadn't died of any complications from his broken ankle. I had seen something in that one instant I'd stood in the hallway with my father's brandy on a tray, Blanche looking down at my father not wringing her gloved hands as I wished to remember, but pressing a rose-dappled throw pillow against his face.

And then the pillow was gone, and I couldn't even be sure I had seen it. I tried to search his room later, but Mrs. Franklin had already tidied everything away. The rose pillows that had been my mother's favorite sat unblemished on the over-plumped wingchair beside the bed, just as they ever had.

I lay in bed all that night, thinking about what I had seen. Of course I had seen nothing. Blanche would never do anything so improper. Of course.

That was when the house first started whispering to me, and I knew I had to leave Storm Break as quickly as I could.

Within a month, I'd found a live-in position teaching art at a girl's school. It paid poorly, and I had no time to myself for art or reading—or even bad dreams. Now the dreams had caught up with me. Maybe Storm Break *was* haunted. Did Father's spirit still wait for me to bring that brandy? Was it the one that had locked me in the bathroom that night or who kept Lillian up all night thumping at her door? Or was it Blanche, furious she was being replaced in Abigail or Frederick's hearts?

I caught up with the housemaid. "You don't really think there are any ghosts at Storm Break, do you, Maureen?"

"I haven't seen any, Miss. Although—" She stopped and gave me an odd look. "It does seem like the pipes have been making more noise since you arrived."

"But that's plumbing, not ghosts."

"Right, Miss. Of course." She bobbed her head unconcernedly. "Who believes in ghosts these days?"

And of course, out here in the sunshine, it was a struggle to believe in ghosts or magic or anything stranger than a portrait sitting session. If I could have stayed out there all day, perhaps then I could have simply enjoyed my family's house and grounds. There was no view imaginable that could rival the view from Storm Break's garden. The little courtyards with their rose-draped trellises framed the blues and grays of both sea and sky, my mother's carefully selected marble railings a white seam stitching the estate to the end of the Earth.

When I was younger I had leaned over the hand-carved balustrades and peered down the golden stone of the cliff face, had imagined how easy it would be to soar over the edge and float down to the foam below. The sea at Storm Break's feet was never quiet. It spat at the stone and churned against the cliffs, in its fury beating its surface to cream. The peaceful poise of the distant waters was a mask for the true tumult ever-seething beneath its surface.

Abigail seized my free hand, emboldened, perhaps, by Maureen's diminishing figure and my silence. "What are you doing out here, June-a-moon?"

Where she had gotten my brother's pet name for me, I couldn't imagine. "Sketching Lillian. You remember."

"Pewter says we should be out in the woods today."

"Pewter isn't in charge. Your papa is."

She stepped in front of me, blocking the path. "The garden doesn't like us to be here," she whispered. "Can't you feel it?"

We had never spent time in the garden, not even once in all our rambles. I shifted the canvas so I could reach for her hand.

"I used to play out here all the time as a little girl. Maybe it will be all right if you're with me."

She shook her head. The arm clutching Pewter squeezed so hard the poor stuffed thing nearly bent in half. "That was before Mother planted the roses. Before the golden child."

I pulled her closer. "What do you mean, Abigail? Golden child?"

She yanked her hand free. "I can't tell, I mustn't, I won't!"

"Abigail!"

But she was already squeezing through the boxwood hedge, twigs snapping and crashing behind her. The gardener would have his work cut out for him repairing it.

"She's always been a difficult child." Frederick appeared on the path in front of me, his hair like embers in the late morning sun. I hoped the strong light didn't flatten Lillian's features; perhaps tomorrow I could convince her to get outside before the sun passed over the house.

I brought my mind back to the child. It bothered me to see Abigail running wild again. I thought something had changed inside her, had softened and warmed, and now I saw misery peeking out again, its slitted eyes just as fierce as before. "She reminds me of myself."

"Oh no, dear June. You were never disobedient." He gave a throaty little chuckle. "June, Moon, June, always floating about, watching us all with the sweetness of an angel."

I supposed he was right. While my parents lived, I never broke a rule, never breathed a word, never did anything. Except, as he said, watch people. Even when I thought I saw Blanche stooped over my father with that pillow, I had played by the rules of the house. All these years later, I still hadn't spoken a word against her, not even to my poet.

My brother patted my shoulder. "I see Lillian making her way toward us. I'll just give her a kiss before I head out the door."

"Are you headed to the sawmill?"

"The shipyard in Charleston. There has been some trouble in my absence, I am sorry to say."

"What happened?"

But Lillian approached, and if Frederick heard my question, it could not distract him from her beauty.

Gone was the small sturdy being in men's underwear; here floated a butterfly, a fairy, a honey-haired queen out of troubadour song. The tasseled green silk shawl around her shoulders waved in the breeze like fern fronds.

Frederick pressed a kiss upon her and murmured endearments before excusing himself. Lillian took a tentative step toward me. Only at an arm's length could I see the smudges of tiredness beneath her eyes.

"Thanks for helping me last night."

"You're welcome." It had been a great deal easier to talk to her when she was dressed like a farmboy.

"It was just the wind or something, wasn't it?" The words rushed together. "Wind can make a door act like that, right?"

I opened my mouth, but Maureen was calling: "The easel's all ready for you!"

Lillian's eyes rolled, and I stifled a laugh, and my mind straightened itself out of the honeyed, green silk folds I'd wrapped it in.

"Let's get this canvas into place and start sketching."

She took one side of the canvas. "Let me help."

Her assistance made it ever so much easier carrying that awkward thing across the uneven bricks of the courtyard. We did have to stop to untangle her dress from the claws of the pinkest rose, but after that, yes, it was easier.

AT LUNCH, THE house closed in on me as I sat in the dining room, alone save for Mrs. Franklin's eyes, as watchful as my mother's had ever been. She said nothing as she passed through, although I heard her scolding Maureen in the hallway. If either Lillian or Abigail had been with me, I wouldn't have even noticed Mrs. Franklin, her lips pressed into a sharp line, a seam ruched with a lifetime of judgment. Had she ever laughed? Had she ever smiled? I couldn't imagine it. But how often had I really noticed her, except for those moments where she wanted to be seen, unsmiling and watchful?

I pushed aside my empty plate and retreated to the library.

After Blanche's arrival at Storm Break, the library had become my sanctuary. Neither my mother nor her cousin-turned-protégée took any interest in that room. They had parties to plan, guests to fete. They were always laughing together, whether planning a trip to San Francisco or an expedition to Coos Bay. They had become good friends long before my brother knew he wanted to marry Blanche.

In those years, people filled the house. Monsieur Alain engaged seven kitchen assistants. The tennis courts—the ones Frederick so recently built over with his experimental dairy—were never empty. The chauffeur kept three men just to ready the fleet of cars, and the gardener had to hire an assistant.

I suppose those were the brightest times for Storm Break, those two years Mother finally managed to push Storm Break into the center of the world. Governors and bankers came; opera singers and novelists; lumber and railroad barons and the first industrialists of the West. But while Mother and Blanche enjoyed the fruits of their labors, I became quieter and more nervous. There was no place in such a beautiful realm for an ugly duckling like me. I escaped to my daydreams and to the world of books.

Today the library welcomed me as it always had. The sun dazzled motes of dust in the gilded air as I made a slow circuit of its beloved shelves. So many volumes, leather-bound and handsome, old friends all. I wasn't sure which one might comfort me at the moment, though. I had realized over lunch that I missed the school very much. There was always something new to read or do there; my students were always inventing some fresh way to talk or walk or joke. I missed the boardinghouse, missed sitting around the table drinking thick, hot coffee over the afternoon papers. I missed my poetess with her serious eyes and long, nimble fingers.

Footsteps sounded behind me, and I spun around, hopeful. "Hello?"

Not even a servant passed by in the empty hall. I turned back to the bookshelves. I could feel eyes follow my arm as I reached out for a volume of Jules Verne.

I glanced back over my shoulder. The feeling someone watched me did not fade.

I hurried upstairs with the book under my arm and wished someone, anyone, had been there in the library doorway. I did not wish to be alone anymore today. My bedroom door caught on something, and I had to work to push it open.

"Hello, Aunt June."

Abigail huddled on my bedroom floor, quilts and sheets tented around her so that her face barely showed.

I sat down beside her, suddenly relieved. "Hello, Abbie."

Her face vanished. "No one's ever called me that before."

I could barely hear her. "Do you like it?"

The blankets bobbed.

"Me, too."

Pewter's face wormed itself out of the pile. A sticky purple spot stained his muzzle. "We're sorry we runned off."

"It's all right, Pewter. I know you don't like the gardens."

The toy's head shook a strong negative. "They don't like *us*."

"That's what I meant."

Abigail pushed back the blankets. Her hair stood up in a frizz of brown. "Why do you think the gardens hate us so much, Aunt June? More than the house, even."

I pushed myself close enough to put my arms around her. Her hair tickled my chin. "I don't know, Abbie-girl. I wish it would stop."

"Me, too. I wish we could go back to being outside all the time." She leaned against me. She smelled cozily of crushed ferns and seaside, the faint animal stink of damp child. I had never imagined holding a child like this. I had never imagined wanting to.

"Your father wants me to paint his new wife," I reminded her. "We want to make him happy, don't we?"

She jumped to her feet, nearly knocking me over. "I just remembered. I've got something for you!"

I got up. "What is it?"

She went to the bed and wormed her hand under the mattress. "A surprise."

Whatever she'd hidden in there, once she found it, she tucked it behind her back, smirking. Then something turned her attention to the window, and she headed to it with a frown.

"What is it?"

"Mr. Watson." She tapped the glass, and I pressed close to look outside with her.

"What's he doing here?" I mused. "Frederick's at the shipyards."

"What's he doing with *her*?" Abigail countered.

I pushed myself back from the window as if distance could ease the strangeness. Lillian stood stiff beside Watson's car, her face unreadable. Watson murmured in her ear. I couldn't imagine that bristly mustache coming so close to me, its rough hairs grinding against my flesh. My dry-rasped hands tightened themselves against my elbows, wrapping myself against the seamy presence of that man.

He opened the car door and slipped inside. If he said something else to Lillian as he did so, I couldn't see. I had eyes only for Lillian's face, its stone beginning to sag.

Then Abigail tugged me back to her blanket next. "Forget about them. Come see your present."

I tried not to look over my shoulder, but I couldn't help seeing the sky fill up the mullions, the dark clouds of a rain squall pushing in at the edge. I dropped onto the blanket nearly too tired to humor my charge.

"I fixed it," she explained. "I practiced on Pewter a little first."

I took the small leather book, its black binding zig-zagged with brown darning wool. Abigail's stitches could not obscure the damage inflicted upon my poor old sketchbook, the long jagged tear where some cruel force had wrenched it in half. The cover showed other violence—jabs, gouges, battered corners. Even closed, I could see pages had been ripped out, leaving ragged stubs.

I folded back the cover, releasing the smell of wood glue. Abigail had worked very hard to repair this.

It was a surprise to see her on the first page, the lines clearly in my own hand but showing a teenaged lack of confidence. I'd drawn Abigail at perhaps a year-and-a-half, her baby face softer but still recognizable under a beribboned bonnet.

My eyes went to the bookshelf with its gaps. "Where did you find this?"

"The attic." She reached out to stroke my hair. "After Mrs. Franklin moved Mother's things up there, I found all sorts of treasures."

"This was in your mother's things? Damaged like this?"

Abigail twisted a lock of my hair around her finger, her eyes dreamy. "I love your hair, Auntie. Do you think mine will ever be as pretty as yours?"

I flipped a few pages further, wondering just what I had sketched that had driven Blanche to such a rage. She had hated me, there at the end. Did she know? Did she suspect that I had seen her with that rose-patterned pillow? My hand trembled a little as I turned the pages.

Here I had sketched Frederick leaning against a new car. Here, Abigail in the garden. Abigail with a doll. Abigail in a pram. Abigail holding Blanche's gloved hand, the mother's hair piled tall and dressed for a party, her high-waisted gown doing little to hide the grand curve of her belly.

I had forgotten about the second baby. First an apoplexy had taken Maman, and then the baby arrived, stillborn, and then Blanche had begun fighting with my father over every little thing. If those times had been dark for me, they must have been even darker for Blanche.

"June? Are you ignoring me?" Abigail tugged at my hair.

"Just thinking, little one. Get my hairbrush from the vanity and I'll brush your hair—make it shiny like mine."

She jumped up to grab the brush. I was glad to sit quietly, my mind free, my own. It hurt me to remember Blanche, her little cruelties, her disdain. But in truth she hadn't always been the quick-tempered woman who spent hours arguing with Father and Mrs. Franklin, ripping up the gardens and redecorating rooms. She had never been kind, but she had never boiled over or seethed. Even after Mother died—Blanche's only friend in all of Oregon—Blanche had focused on the pleasure of society.

It was the baby that had changed her, and I had forgotten that. She had gone from unpleasant to nightmarish in the course of a few short weeks, and I could only truly remember the nightmare.

Abigail snuggled warm against me and I wondered, had the baby been simply stillborn, as my brother had told me, or was there something more to its loss? And just what had happened in this house while I blinded myself with the library?

"Aunt June?" Abigail tugged my elbow.

"Yes, dear one?"

"You haven't thanked me for your present yet."

I patted her shoulder. My hand looked red and chapped on her yellow sundress. It made me want to open the sketchbook again and see what Blanche's hands looked like. But flipping through, I found my memory was right: Blanche never went gloveless, not even inside the house. That hadn't seemed strange to me at the time, not growing up with Maman and her distaste for being seen with cracked, unladylike hands. It had never occurred to me that perhaps Blanche wore gloves for the same reason. Ichthyosis ran in families, after all, and she was our cousin. I couldn't imagine Blanche allowing herself even a single blemish.

"*June!*" Abigail tugged harder. Behind my head, the pipes gave an unusually loud gurgle.

"Yes, dear." I patted her shoulder again. "I'm so very grateful for my present."

EIGHT

THE *SNICK* OF the bedroom door opening woke me. I rubbed
sleep's confusion from my eyes, the pattern of darkness
resolving itself into shapes. Feet padded in the hallway.

"Abigail?"

I switched on the light, bringing clarity to the emptiness of the
floor. Only Pewter sat in Abigail's blanket nest, his eyes dark, the
crooked stitches of his mouth uneasy.

I found my robe on the foot of my bed and stepped into the
hallway. No light or sounds from the bathroom to my left. My
bare toes dug into the rasping wool of the runner. "Abigail?" I
whispered again.

Downstairs, a door clicked open. I hurried to the staircase.

"Is everything all right?"

I waved back at Lillian, not sure how to answer. The
bannister groaned beneath my hand. All around me the tiny
noises of the house seemed to shift in tone and pitch, their
intonation higher, tighter, more excited than usual. Abigail never
woke up in the night. The house knew it.

Shoes sounded behind me, but I didn't look back. I cut through the main hallway to the sun room, running now. I hadn't heard the shush and drag of the French doors, but I knew it was coming. The house moved as it had in the bathroom that first night, the wood groaning and popping its message, the taps shrieking their song of deliverance.

The French doors slammed shut ahead of me. I grabbed the bronze handles and yanked. For a moment they resisted. Then Lillian was beside me, her hands pushing down on mine with a power outsized for her slight body.

The doors burst open and I stumbled out onto the brick patio. The rain had stopped for the moment, but clouds still obscured the sky, and the wind pushed against me with cold, hard hands.

"Abigail?"

Lillian grabbed my arm. "There!"

My heart lurched. Abigail twirled in a circle beside the white fountain, her nightgown's hem ballooning around her legs. I leaped over the boxwoods, running toward her. She spun away, the wind pushing her down the path toward the sea view.

"Abigail, wake up!"

Lillian gave a shout of pain, and I risked a glance over my shoulder. The climbing rose, the neatly trellised pink one, had caught her around the leg just as it had this morning.

This time, I didn't stop for Lillian. The sea roared below us, hungry and angry.

The craggy limb of another, thicker rose bush caught in my dressing gown and I yanked free. Why hadn't the gardener pruned the damned things?

Abigail spun, wobbled, hit the line of boxwoods and ricocheted, wind and sleep spinning her farther down the path, farther from me. The low line of white balustrade lay only a few feet beyond us, one more turn in the brick path. I pushed my legs faster, the bricks rasping on my naked feet.

Then the rain began, a fierce, cold rain like claws raking my body. I skidded on dirt become mud. I flailed a moment, my eyes fixed on Abigail's small form. Then I was upright, arms pumping, going over the hedge to block Abigail's path.

"Abigail!" I grabbed her outstretched arms.

"I can't stop," she yelled. Her legs kicked and stomped, her body twisted. "I can't wake up!"

Her skin, wet and clammy, slid out of my grip. I caught onto her hair. A wave struck the base of the cliff hard enough to send spray over us.

Then Lillian was there, her stupid union suit sodden in the rain, jumping as I had jumped, crashing into Abigail and throwing her to the ground. The pair tumbled sideways, smashing into the balustrade, and I screamed.

I caught them both, pressing them down into the mud, driving my fingers into their clothes. I yanked and I pulled and Lillian helped, the two of us stronger together, and Abigail going stiller and stiller.

"I'm cold, auntie." She burrowed into my body. "Why am I outside and why am I so cold and where did the music go?"

"It's okay, sweetie. Let's get you inside and warm." I hoisted her to her feet.

"What music?" Lillian asked.

"The party music, of course," Abigail murmured, her eyes drooping with sleep. She yawned. "It was such a nice party, too. I didn't want it to end."

The hairs on the back of my neck prickled at that. How many times had I heard my mother say the exact same thing at the end of a long, brilliant night? Her portrait sneered at us as we crept up the staircase.

I bundled Abigail in my own spare nightgown, far too large for her. I pulled the blankets up to her chin. "Are you all right, Abigail?"

Her eyelids gave a little flutter, but she was already asleep. I shivered and rubbed the damp sleeves of my dressing gown. If it hadn't been for the cold and wet, I could almost believe nothing had happened, that we had all been caught up in a terrible, terrible dream. But I could smell the salt spray on my hair and clothes, feel its chill against my skin. It had been real, all right. Something had called Abigail out to the edge of the cliff, and Lillian had helped me save her.

Shivering, I tiptoed back into the hallway. The door to Frederick's old room stood open, and Lillian sat on the edge of the bed, watching me. She had changed out of the union suit into a man's flannel shirt and dungarees.

"You're all wet."

I rubbed my arms. "It feels like winter in here."

She held up a black and green dressing gown, all satin and lace, the kind of thing a Hollywood star might have slipped into while deciding which lipstick to wear to her gala. "Put this on."

I had to laugh. "It'll never fit. Besides, it's far too pretty."

Lillian slid off the bed and pulled me by the wrist into the room, kicking the door shut behind us. "You deserve pretty, June." She had a towel, too, sitting next to that ridiculously luxurious gown. I took that. The room smelled different than it had when I'd first arrived in the house. The camphor had dissipated, replaced by some heavy sweet smell I couldn't quite place.

"What were you doing up?"

"I don't sleep." She dropped back onto the bed. "Your brother wants me to stay in that room next to his, but I can hear it breathing at me."

I paused toweling my hair. "Why don't you just sleep with Frederick?"

She lay back on the bed and stretched herself like a starfish. She hadn't bothered with the buttons at the bottom of her shirt; it spread open, exposing the dimple of her navel in the creamy expanse of her belly. I had to look away from it. She was my brother's wife.

I pushed on. "I don't think I'll be able to sleep tonight. The way she moved out there, Lillian." I caught myself shivering again and began scrubbing my arms with the towel. "It was like a nightmare. A waking nightmare."

She rolled onto her belly and opened the nightstand on the far side of the bed. Something rustled in there; something clanked. I heard the scratch and hiss of a match.

"What are you doing?"

"I know all about nightmares." She pushed herself up to sit cross-legged, holding a small golden pipe. It reminded me of my mother's bronze dragon-dogs. "Champagne helps. This is better."

Lillian took a long drag on the pipe and held the smoke in her lungs, watching me with eyes that saw something very distant.

She let out the smoke in a soft, sweet-scented breath.

"What is that?"

"It'll help you sleep. You can't let all these ghosts and nightmares keep you from sleeping."

"Lillian."

She leaned back against the headboard. "You're shivering."

"I'll be all right."

"Take off your wet things and put on my dressing gown, June. You don't want to catch a cold."

I stood up. The buttons squeaked in their damp buttonholes. I turned my back to her, drawing the soaked nightgown over my head. There was no place to put it except over the back of the overstuffed chair where Frederick used to sit and read to me. I kept one arm crooked around my breasts as I reached for the dressing gown. She was watching me.

"You're beautiful, June."

I tied the gown at my waist, my eyes rolling. "You're ridiculous."

"I know beautiful. It's my job to be beautiful." She took a smaller puff, her eyes roaming down the neckline of the gown, the lace at its sides, the place at the thigh where it didn't quite meet. She was thinner than me, after all. Thinner and smaller in every direction, except the eyes and the mouth. No one had ever had such a rich, full mouth. "It's why your brother noticed me in the first place."

"How could he not?" I perched on the edge of the bed, hiding my rough hands beneath my legs. I could almost feel pretty with her looking at me like that—and my hands hidden.

She took another pull and put the pipe down on a plate she'd brought out of the nightstand. "The Chinese did us all a favor when they brought opium to this country."

"Opium?"

"The doctor prescribed it for me once." She gave a dry laugh. "Doctor. He was the one who started Mother's little parties. He knew all the right people to invite. He took care of everything."

I scooted closer to her. "What do you mean?"

Her eyes closed. "I had to get out of that house." Her head turned, but her eyes didn't open. "Frederick was so, so nice. He didn't know what kind of party he'd been invited to.

When Ebenezer Watson told him to visit Mother's house, Frederick had no idea what he was in for. And so maybe I tricked him. Maybe I told him he was special."

I didn't dare breathe. What was she telling me?

Her eyes shot open. "I had to do it, June. I couldn't stay there any longer, not even with all the opium in San Francisco."

Ebenezer Watson. I remembered the black-and-red matchbook in his car and the way he'd whispered in Lillian's ear as if he had every right to press his greasy mustache into her flesh. As if he already knew it quite well.

I put my trembling arm around her shoulder and pressed my cheek to hers. Her eyes felt wet and hot. "You're all right now, Lillian. Everything will be all right."

Her hand was warm and strong as it slid down from my cheek to my breast and cupped it. "I know," she whispered, and then her mouth was hot on mine and my hands were on her sleek, smooth skin. An image of Frederick sitting at my father's desk flickered in my mind's eye, his kind, handsome face smiling up at me, but then Lillian shoved me backward onto the bed, and the impact drove his smile away. I could only gasp as she yanked the lacy dressing gown up over my hips. Then she plunged into the heart of me, and, and I couldn't think of anything except her.

AND SO WE were joined, Lillian, right or wrong.

You've never once doubted our love, but then, you never loved my brother, and you never knew what it was like to have one. He had tried so hard to protect me from my mother, and what did I do to return that favor, but to steal you away from him? You say you are as much to blame as I am, but I cannot see fault in you. Alone with all those men, you had only yourself to love all those years, and you learned to reach for what you needed.

My mother taught me many things, Lillian: that I was ugly, that my skin was shame, that I did not belong in the smooth, perfect walls of Storm Break, no matter how much it felt like a part of me. But what she taught me best was to only look at beautiful things, and never, ever touch them.

But I will touch you now, and then I will close my eyes. Tomorrow is soon enough to look at the past again.

LATER THAT NIGHT, I slipped out of Lillian's bed—as I have just slipped out of ours—and went to my own room. I did not sleep. And when morning came, I gathered myself for a day of spreading both smiles and lies across my face.

In the bathroom, the door refused to close. So I propped my sketchbook against it before I went to the counter. The sweet stink of Lillian's pipe smoke clung to my hair; the flower of her skin and sex perfumed everywhere else. I scrubbed my hands and face with soap, once, twice, again, until my skin stung. The pipes below the sink growled to themselves, or maybe to me. *Your brother's wife.*

I patted my face dry and stared at myself in the mirror. Had my eyes always been so large? My lips so pink? Even my hair looked too shiny, too smooth. I almost looked like the sort of woman who could wear a lace dressing gown as if it were ordinary garb.

My fingers trembled as I scooped balm from the tin and began working it into my hands. They weren't the hands of the shiny, big-eyed stranger in the mirror. They were ugly, coarse. The lines of my palms were the same rough white as the oyster shell drive. Working hands, that's what my mother had called them. No matter how much Frederick and I scrubbed and scoured, we could not get rid of our working hands and scaling arms. What a disappointment we had been. And now look: I worked for my living. My hands did work.

But I liked living that way. I liked *working.*

Breathing deep the lavender smell of the cream, I readied myself for work. I gathered my sketchbook, my sack of pencils and pastels. I would probably use none of them today, but I would only know when I looked over the sketching I'd done yesterday. I hoped to be able to begin the underpainting today.

The painting. I could focus on the painting, on the work my good, kind brother had given me. I choked back tears as I opened the door. The house breathed quietly around me, its pipes and floors waiting for me to misbehave.

Frederick swept past Lillian's closed bedroom door, smiling as ever. I met him at the top of the staircase.

"You look as ready for breakfast as I am, dear Moon." He pulled me into an embrace, kissing my cheek. A few yellow flakes clung to the sides of his red hair, like scales shed from some monstrous goldfish. My mother would have made him wash them away.

"Famished."

He set his hand on the small of my back, urging me down the stairs. I could remember my father doing the same thing. But at the landing, a stepladder nearly blocked the staircase. Mrs. Franklin stood at the top, absorbed in the play of her duster's feathers against the surface of my mother's portrait. A mobcap covered her usually severe bun, and for a moment I saw the woman she must have been when she first came to Storm Break—the dimpled cheeks, the soft round eyes, the cheerfully upturned nose. Then she noticed us below, and her face closed up tight.

"Mr. Vogel. Miss Vogel."

Frederick shook his finger at her. "You work too hard, Mrs. Franklin. It's Saturday."

"I dust this painting every Saturday, Mr. Vogel. Rain or shine."

"But I'm taking this painting down, you know. I told you. I'll send it to a conservator in San Francisco to have it properly cleaned before I find another place for it."

"I dust it every Saturday, sir. Just as your mother would have had it."

He could only nod again. "Well, keep up the good work." He steered me around the stepladder, murmuring in my ear: "She's a difficult woman, but there's no complaining about her work ethic."

I raised an eyebrow, remembering what he had said about Abigail yesterday. "It seems this house is full of difficult people, isn't it?" Our feet tapped on the parquet floors of the main hallway.

"Indeed." He sighed. "Yesterday Lillian told me she found a slug in her bed. Can you imagine? I knew Abigail would have a hard time with this, but a slug seems excessive."

He clearly knew nothing about Abigail's more unusual abilities. Slugs were only the beginning of what she could do.

"Abigail will get used to things," I reassured him. I tried to step toward the dining room, but his hand on my back pushed me toward the sun room.

"Distract me a moment, June-a-Moon. Show me what you've done on the portrait so far."

"I've only just started," I warned him. "It took most of the morning to work out the pose, the background—"

He waved his free hand impatiently. "I know your work. I trust your instincts. I just want a little sunshine this morning."

I stopped in the doorway of the sun room. "What's wrong?"

I studied his face closely. It wasn't just the dandruff, I saw now. The skin around his mouth had gone patchy, red and irritated; his eyes lacked their usual brightness. He hadn't slept well last night.

I thought of the way I had spent the night and felt my stomach twist around itself. My brother's wife. His very newlywed wife.

The words took their time forming. "The shipyards," he finally said.

"What about them?"

He forced a smile. "My interests lie in agriculture and forestry. What of it to cut ties with an industry that fails to provoke my imagination?"

"Are the shipyards failing?" He was walking away from me, striding into the sun room where the easel and canvas sat shrouded in linen. "Frederick?"

"It's a dying industry," he said, glancing over his shoulder. "Who wants steamers when we've got trains and cars?" His hand reached out to the fabric cover. "May I?"

"But Frederick—"

He hadn't waited for me to answer, and the sight of my work stopped the words in my mouth, surprise and dismay bleeding them into an ineffectual gasp.

"What?" Frederick asked, his voice hollow. "What?"

I rushed forward, my hands going out to my slashed and fraying canvas. Even the wooden stretchers had been broken. I couldn't help the pricking in my eyes, my chest.

"Who would do something like this?" he whispered.

The sides of the canvas showed jabs, rips, nasty little gashes. I had seen this before on the notebook Abigail had found in the attic.

I pulled the flaps of fabric together as if I could smooth Lillian's face back into place, reattach her to the background of the world.

"Abigail."

I had never heard Frederick's voice like that—low, hard. My father's voice when he told Blanche to get rid of her roses.

"No, Frederick, not Abigail."

But did I know it wasn't Abigail? Did I really know that she had found my notebook already cut and slashed? Didn't it seem just as likely that she had made the cuts herself?

He brushed aside my arm. "Don't defend her, June. This can't go unpunished."

A gasp sounded from the doorway, and Abigail rushed past me. "I didn't do it!"

He spun to face his daughter, the back of his neck filling up with red. "You little liar."

"Frederick!" I tried to grab his arm, but my memory of last night weighed down my hand. She had walked right through this room to get outside. Had there been enough time for her to do this while I stumbled down the stairs looking for her? Had her whole dance in the garden last night been some kind of cover for her misdeeds?

"Aunt June, please!"

Frederick grabbed her by the wrist.

"Abigail?" I couldn't believe it of her. Couldn't not believe it.

"You're going to your room, you little brat, and you're going to stay there until you know better."

She gave a little shriek—was it pain? rage? despair?—as he dragged her out of the room. Their feet thudded down the corridor beyond the sun room. Heading for the back stairs. The servants' quarters.

I had to reach out for the back of the nearest chair to support my sagging knees. He was shutting Abigail in the attic again. He was shutting her away from me.

"Serves you right."

I could barely hear that soft hiss from the doorway, but the house itself seemed to echo the words.

Mrs. Franklin folded her arms across her chest, her smile all victory.

NINE

MY FEET FOUND their way into town. I still held my sketchbook, my pencil case, and when I began to smell Anderson's Bakery, I remembered I had a few nickels tucked in with the art supplies. I went inside and bought a roll for breakfast.

The baker's wife gave me a cup of coffee without my even asking. That morning must have showed on my face.

I ate with one hand, sketched with the other, as if my pencil could draw something out of the pit of my stomach to make room for breakfast, for the ordinary, the good. Maybe that was what sketching always meant to me: a purgative.

Perhaps that's why I threw myself into art after Father died. The wrongness of that moment had pierced me to the core, the wound putrefying as it grew deeper. It had seemed impossible that I had really seen Blanche standing over my father with a pillow, pushing him down, down, down into his bed. It made no sense.

But some part of me was sure she had.

Tears rolled down my cheeks, salting my roll. I had run away rather than believe my own eyes. I had let her get away with murder.

I covered my mouth so no sounds would give away my feelings, but the tears and the puffs of air—*the sobs, they're called sobs*, some funny part of my mind reminded me—wouldn't stop.

I couldn't remember the last time I had cried. Really cried. Not for Father, not for Maman, not since perhaps the day Maman and Mrs. Franklin gathered up my dolls and burned them with the trash, just for the crime of playing out two girls kissing. Even then, I could only truly remember the pain, not the tears.

Oh, Lillian, maybe that was why I hadn't been willing to trust the certainty in my gut, those eight years ago. Maybe I'd spent so long denying everything I felt and thought and saw that I could only think about what looked right, and what people thought, and what they expected.

Certainly at the time, I couldn't have told Frederick. He might not have loved Blanche—not as he seemed to love Lillian—but he had idolized her for what she was: the living embodiment of the world his mother had built around him. To criticize her would have hurt him beyond all repair. He was not like me. He had no drawings to drive the rot out of his wounds. His mind was tender and fragile, like his heart.

Like his heart. I covered my face in my cool hands. What would it do to Frederick if he ever discovered what I had done with Lillian last night? Such thoughts would break him.

Voices, climbing higher, pulled my attention from my own troubles.

"I *know* you're a good worker, Andrew. I know you and your wife are the very salt of the Earth. You don't think I'd leave little Tommy with you two if I didn't think you were the right sort?"

I had never heard the baker's wife sound anything less than jovial. Her hands twisted in her apron, her cheeks splotching red.

The man she addressed, Andrew—I recognized him from the mill. The colored log truck driver Abigail and I had watched. He had his straw hat in his hands, imploring the woman.

For a moment, I was just a little girl again, sitting in the garden with my lessons, pencil in hand, as quiet as a child could be. My mother stood beside the boxwoods, addressing the gardener. He had held his hat just like this man, a dark-skinned stranger standing three cautious feet behind him.

There's just no place in polite society for them, she had said. My pencil had copied the words into the corner of my schoolbook beneath a sketch of a flower. *You understand, don't you? My husband would never allow someone like* that *to work here.*

The past snapped inside me, along with the charcoal stick in my hand. The words *no place in polite society* filled the page in black smudges.

"I can't keep driving for Murphy," the black man said in a soft voice. "The men at the mill have it in for me. That Ebenezer Watson—"

"Will still have it in for you if you work here." Mrs. Anderson reached out to him, her hand squeezing his shoulder not unkindly. "He's been bothering Karl about going to those awful Klan meetings in Coos Bay. He's got his eye on us. And you know too much of our work starts before sun up. Yarrow's no place for your kind before sunup."

He fixed her a hard look. "I thought we were the same kind, Mrs. Anderson."

The man strode out of the bakery, head high as he clapped his boater back on it. He glanced my way as he passed by. I tried to smile. He didn't.

"You heard all that, I suppose." Mrs. Anderson appeared beside me. She put a plate on my table, one of her oversized cinnamon rolls dripping with vanilla glaze. Its sweetness rose up between us, nearly solid. "I'd appreciate if you didn't mention anything about that conversation to your brother."

"My brother?"

"Or Mr. Watson, neither." She gave the roll a tiny push toward me. "Please."

It was a long walk home, and upon my arrival, I only paused a minute to drop my sketchbook and pencils in my room before I went to find Beamon. Maureen could do nothing; Mrs. Franklin I could not even talk to; but Beamon might help me. He had always treated me with a respect that bordered on kindness.

I found him in his office going over the house accounts. Although I hadn't spoken, Beamon turned around in his desk chair. The glasses perched on the tip of his nose changed his face, deepened the lines around his eyes, the sadness in their pale depths. He was getting old, I saw now. My father enjoyed telling the story of Beamon's first day on the job, arriving at the nearly empty house to find my mother still giving orders to the workers as she pretended she was not giving birth. Beamon had driven the twenty-five miles into Coos Bay to bring her a doctor. He had been in America all of a month.

"Can I help you, Miss Vogel?"

"Is Abigail still shut up in her room? I need to see her."

He adjusted his glasses. "I'm sorry, miss. Mr. Vogel left explicit orders not to let anyone in."

"But Beamon—"

He raised a hand, cutting me off. "I cannot." He unfolded himself from his desk chair. His black suit hung more loosely on him than I remembered. "It is not a choice that perhaps you or I might have made, but he is her father, and master of this house."

So we were alike, we two, bound by the rules of the house to see and to judge but to have our hands tied. I thanked him and went out in the hall. In this world, this place, I was entitled to enjoy the fruits of my family's wealth and power but to have none of my own. Beamon could at least carry the keys to this castle and know his place in the structure of it all. I had merely Frederick's generosity to give me place and purpose, and that could only take me so far.

At that moment, Lil, I very nearly walked back outside. At the boarding house, I was poor, but I was free, and to be caged again after living free felt like a hand closing tight around my windpipe. Like a rose-patterned pillow pressed into my face. In those few seconds, I would have done anything to put Storm Break behind me. I had to put my hand on the wall and gasp against my bonds.

I know now that I couldn't have run away, that I was truly shackled to that place. Love held me with a fastness more powerful than fear or shame or anger. You and Abigail were already my family, my heart, my soul, my entirety. Only Storm Break kept me from seeing it.

So instead of running out the front door as I wished, I went up the back stairs and found my way to Abigail's door. I shook the handle as hard as I could.

"Abigail?"

Silence.

"Abigail!"

Something slithered behind the door. I could picture her creeping across the floor in her nest of blankets, her face invisible, her hands splayed out from beneath the layers like the bleached limbs of a desiccated starfish.

The rustling settled into a listening silence. I lowered myself to the ground and rested my cheek against the wood. The flaking paint pressed roughly into my skin. "I can't get the door open. I tried to come visit, but no one will let me."

"It's very dark in here." Was that her voice, or only the rustle of the blankets? The tightness in my throat grew stronger. I wished I could kick down the door and take her out of that room. We could run away together, the three of us going north to Portland, farther north to Seattle, even all the way to Canada where no Vogel had ever set foot.

"I don't want to go anyplace with Lillian," she said as if my wish had passed through my skull and vibrated across the closed door.

"Once you get to know Lillian, you'll like her better. She helped save you last night. You should remember that."

"But she's stealing you from me." The door thudded as some part of her shifted against it. "She took my papa, and now she's taking you."

"People can love more than one person, Abbie. It's not like our hearts only have one key."

"Maybe. Maybe there are no keys, like here in Storm Break. All the doors are locked in this house."

Footsteps thudded down the hallway, but no one appeared. I could feel the house breathing around me, its timbers shifting as it waited for me to answer.

"Do you think the doors lock themselves? Is it the house, Abbie? Or is it someone else?"

"Isn't it all the same?" The doorknob rattled above my head.

It could have been Abigail. It could have been the house.

"Before you came, the house only dreamed about doing bad things," she whispered. "If things happened, they happened because someone else wanted what the house wanted.

Before you came, I almost felt safe."

I sat up straight, staring at the door as if it could show me her face. "What do you mean?"

The door remained blank. Even the blankets stayed silent.

"Tell me what you mean, Abigail."

"Why'd you wake it up, Aunt June? Why?" I thought she said, but it could have been the pipes or the wind beneath the eaves.

Thudding like footsteps sounded down the empty hallway again. The door groaned. I got to my feet. I could not keep sitting there, the floor shaking beneath me, the walls watching and listening.

"I'm going to talk to your father. He won't keep you in there forever."

I tapped my fingers on the door, the sound standing in for a wave, and saw my hand tremble. It wasn't powerlessness or anger that made it hard to breathe now, but only fear.

All of this could be Abigail, I thought. Hadn't I seen her make that sand pail fly up the path? Hadn't I seen her strike sparks in Ebenezer Watson's hand?

The blankets rustled behind the door. It reminded me very horribly of the sound the blankets made as they slid off my father's lap as he fought for his last breath.

The floor pounded as if an entire herd of elk raced down it.

"You're the one who woke it up," Pewter growled. "You're the one who opened its eyes."

I backed away from the door, unable to talk, unable to breathe. Unable to ask just what had awakened. Or how I had awakened it.

I ATE DINNER alone. Lillian felt unwell, Beamon explained. Frederick had a meeting in Coos Bay.

I remembered Mrs. Anderson mentioning Ebenezer Watson and his meetings in Coos Bay, and I wondered what I would find if I looked in Frederick's closet. Would there be an empty hanger where a white robe and hood ought to hang? The thought made me push aside my unfinished dinner and run to my room.

A box sat on my bed where it should not. It was small, and blue, the kind of neat little box that ought to hold jewelry. An engagement ring, maybe. I didn't want to open it.

I sat on the bed a long moment, and then I did. Only a small glinting of gold lay at the bottom, a tiny mass of something like yellow sand, but coarser, flakier. When I touched it, one of the flakes clung to my finger and stayed there. It looked something like a scale scrubbed from a goldfish or a tiny yellow dragon. It looked like Frederick's dandruff.

I brushed it back into the box and shuddered. The mystery of what it was mattered less than how it had gotten in my room.

My door opened a crack. "June? May I come in?"

At the sound of Lillian's voice, liquid fire ran down my spine. Even if I had wanted to tell her no, I couldn't have. I thrust the box onto my bookshelf.

She stepped into the room, filling it with that too-sweet smell of her pipe. Her eyes shone like polished glass.

"I don't want to pretend to sleep anymore. I don't want to be lonely."

And God help me, what I said was: "I don't want to be lonely, either."

She crawled onto my bed where my hands found her, and my lips, and the whole fierce heat of me. I could only pull her more tightly to my hungry body. There was only sensation. The tumbled-down honey of her hair covered my eyes and made them useless.

I AWOKE IN the night to the sound of a door opening and closing, opening and closing. Something inside the walls whined. I burrowed my head into Lillian's breast.

"Hush, house," I whispered, and as if it had been listening for me, it fell silent.

TEN

First thing that morning, I went upstairs to check on
Abigail. The cracked skin on my hands stung and prickled,
and my shirtwaist chafed against newly dry skin on my shoulder
blades. I could feel the house breathing as I moved. Every door I
passed creaked open and then thudded shut. Every treadon the
staircases echoed my footstep. And though I walked alone, the
fabric of heavy skirts rustled down the hallways.

I found Maureen in the upstairs hallway, nudging an empty
breakfast tray out of her way with her booted foot. She dragged a
trunk behind her; she wore ordinary, even somewhat fashionable
clothes. Without her mobcap, I saw her hair was nearly the same
mousey shade as my own.

"Are you leaving, Maureen?"

She glanced up from the tray, her face full of surprise. "Of
course. You should, too, while you still can." The floor gave a
little tremble, and she closed her eyes as if she might be sick. "It
did that all night long. I think the whole house is going to fall
down."

"I'm sure it's perfectly safe."

"Safe? When I said I was applying for this job, folks told me this place was cursed. I didn't believe them. They said there were ghosts, and I *still* didn't believe them. You show up? Now I believe them!"

I reached for her arm. "Maureen—"

"Don't touch me." She shook off my hand and shoved past me, her trunk rolling over my toes. "I'm done with you Vogels and your wicked house."

I stumbled over some kind of response—although what response could I really make, Lillian, with the house rippling beneath my shoulder—but she had already reached the top of the staircase. I swallowed down unease and turned to Abigail's door. "Abigail? How are you this morning?"

"She's not the only one, you know," Abigail called from inside. "I heard the house talking all night long."

I stooped so I could press my eye to the keyhole. Abigail sat in the center of the room, no blankets, no books, just her and Pewter, purple jam staining their mouths. "Can you open the door?" I whispered.

She turned Pewter in her grasp and looked down at his face. She brought his paws together in a game of patty-cake.

"Did you put something in my room last night?"

"You smell like Lillian," she said. "Pewter says you should leave us alone. The house doesn't like her."

I pulled back from the door. I couldn't help bringing my hands to my nose. Lavender, that was all. I'd washed for a long time after Lillian left me at sunrise.

"I'll talk to you later, Abbie. I love you."

I hadn't expected to say it, but it felt true as it came out.

"I love you," I repeated. The floor lurched beneath me.

Downstairs, someone screamed.

I RAN AS fast as I could, nearly stumbling on the final stretch as the narrow stairs shifted beneath my shoes. I passed Monsieur Alain, jogging from the kitchen; I passed Beamon emerging from the butlery. I had never run so quickly. I skidded around the corner and burst into the entryway.

"Lillian!"

She lay on the bottom stairs of the great staircase, and when she heard my voice, she lifted her head a little. "June. I slipped."

A red dot showed on the front of her white skirt. It began to spread.

I threw myself down beside her. "You're bleeding. Are you hurt?"

"Not me, but the baby."

"Baby? Frederick's baby?"

"Maaaybe," she crooned, her eyes as glossy as they'd been the night before. She hissed against sudden pain. "I had to catch him, didn't I? I couldn't stand to let the doctor at me again with his knitting needles."

"Hush, now." I stroked her cheek. "Someone help us!" I shouted over my shoulder.

And then the thunder of footsteps on the second floor. "Lillian!"

Pain and fear turned Frederick's voice into a roar. He half-leaped down the stairs, dropping to his knees beside Lillian and crushing her hand in his. "Dear one."

"The stairs moved," she murmured. Her face had gone nearly translucent. "I was just walking and then they weren't there any longer."

"Oh, you silly thing. Did you hit your head?" Frederick murmured, pressing kisses to her forehead. He looked wretched, too, the skin on his forehead gone to scales and his eyebrows clotted with yellow flakes. "Did you break anything?"

"Frederick, she's bleeding." The stain nearly covered the front of her skirt.

Frederick's face went gray. "The baby. Oh, Christ. Beamon! Get the doctor!"

He lifted Lillian in his arms and strode up the stairs. A trail of blood drops followed after him like a second set of footprints.

Beneath me, the staircase gave a happy wriggle. I slammed my fist into the banister to shut it up.

A baby. That's why they'd left Mexico early. That's why Frederick hadn't minded her late mornings, the meals she'd missed. It had to be Frederick's baby; I couldn't believe what

Lillian had raved there on the stairs. She'd been smoking instead of taking breakfast. Maybe there was nothing supernatural about Lillian's fall, but only opium.

I hit the banister again. I wouldn't think these things. I had watched doors open and close. Heard floors shake and vibrate. If I knew the house was haunted, I didn't need to doubt the people I loved.

Tin clanged behind me, and I turned to see Mrs. Franklin pulling along a big metal mop bucket. It gave off the pungent tang of Fels-Naptha soap.

"You ought to go rest, Miss Vogel." She gave the wringer a fierce squeeze. "We can take care of everything. We know what to do."

Monsieur Alain stepped up behind her shoulder. For the first time, I realized that the uniforms beneath their white aprons were the same shade of blue as the dress Maman wore in her portrait. They both smiled then, the same quiet smile.

The mop bucket rattled softly. I could not tell if it came from the vibration of the house or if Mrs. Franklin caused it. They felt the same, exactly the same.

When I got to my feet, my legs shook all the way out the front door.

ELEVEN

WHY DID I run away, Lillian? Why did I leave you alone when you were hurt and broken and needed me the most? Because that's what I do. I watch, and I run away.

Writing all this, I see that's how I learned to survive in that house. When Maman would yell at Frederick for the state of his skin, I ran to my bedroom and the company of my dolls. When Father and Blanche fought about the house and the gardens, I ran to the library and hid in the books. And when she killed Father, I ran all the way to Portland.

You told me that until I could stop running away from Storm Break, we would never really be happy. I guess that's why I'm writing this. To turn around and not just *see* Storm Break and what happened to us there, but to understand it.

That afternoon after you fell, I could barely see my own feet through the storm inside me, but I came back to the house when it started to rain. Even under the cover of the trees, the rain had pelted me, soaking through my dress and streaming out my hair. The wind lashed my dress against my legs like a whip.

And though I was soaking wet, I had to stop there on the oyster shell drive. Storm Break stood tall and straight, as if the black claws of the surrounding spruce trees caused it no fear. Its shutters beat against the walls to scare away the wilderness.

The house no longer looked like a flower emerging from the woodland understory but a toadstool sprung fully formed from decay.

Storm Break and I had both started out the products of my parents' wishes, carefully shaped and molded and smoothed into place. We were very nearly twins. But I had failed at being a lady. I was only an art teacher with the hands of a fishwife. And Storm Break had failed at being a home. Under its watchful eyes, only horrible things happened.

I pulled open the front door and stood a moment in the entranceway. The space still smelled, faintly, of Fels-Naptha. In the depths of the house, a clock struck four.

Lillian. I had to find out how she was. Rain dripped from my nose as I ran up the stairs. Something down the hallway lub-dubbed like a heartbeat.

Her door had been propped open between a pair of ottomans, but that did not stop it from beating against its restraints. The walls throbbed to the same double beat. I clambered over the ottoman, barely fitting between door and frame, and felt the doorknob drive into my hip. It was the first time the house had really hurt me. I should have known, Lillian, that it would. But I think perhaps I believed our twinship made me different from everyone else.

Entering the room felt like crossing into the eye of a hurricane. The groaning, the thudding all felt very distant. A sick yellow light filled the space, the sun's healthy glow replaced by the subdued glow of a covered lamp. The wallpaper beside the wooden door frame had begun to peel, revealing black-mottled plaster below. The room stank of things both musty and sweet. I thought of toadstools again. I thought of snakes shedding their skin.

Abigail stood at the head of Lillian's bed, Pewter only inches from Lillian's sleeping face. The purple stains on its face were roses.

"Abigail!"

She glanced up at me. "You really love me? Even though you love Lillian, too?"

I couldn't move. I could only stare at that ugly stuffed creature with its rose-purple spots. "Yes, Abigail," I whispered.

"And she did help me save me the other night?"

"Yes, Abigail."

"You're all wet, June-a-Moon." She brought the stuffed creature's nose down to Lillian's and made a tiny kissing sound.

My legs began to tremble. "I've been outside. Walking."

"It's the first storm of summer."

"I guess so."

Lillian made a little snort. Her legs pedaled and her head twisted on the pillow. Her eyes opened. "June? Is that you?"

I hurried to her side. "I'm right here, darling."

Her eyes sagged, then opened wide. "You've got to talk to Watson. I'm out of the good stuff."

"That can all wait until you feel better, Lil. You just rest now."

"How can I rest without it?" But her eyes had shut again. "Can't sleep…"

We watched her a moment as her breathing settled into regularity. I supposed the doctor had given her something to make her rest.

Abigail brushed Lillian's hair back from her cheek. "She doesn't look so fancy right now, does she?"

The house blew cold against my neck as I leaned over the bed. Lillian lay there so pale and still, her eyelashes smiles of russet against her gray-smudged skin. I hadn't noticed that before, how her lashes matched Frederick's hair note for note. They were such a pretty couple. I swallowed down the lump in my throat. I should leave them. I should leave this house.

The house blew colder still.

"I don't think Lillian's fancy at all," I managed to say. "I think she tries because it makes your father happy."

"I know what that's like." She looked up at me then, and the rims of her nostrils were red with invisible tears. "You really, really love me, Aunt June?"

I grabbed her to me. "Yes, Abbie! I love you more than anything. I wish you were my own little girl so I never had to leave you."

She wriggled free of my embrace. "You got me wet!"

I couldn't help laughing. "I guess I'm soaked."

Lillian twisted in her bed. "Watson," she murmured. "Have to…Watson." She gave a little snore and went silent again.

Abigail took my hand and kissed the top of it. "You can go get dry, Auntie. I'll look after Lillian."

I squeezed her hand and took a few steps toward the door. "You don't have to, you know. She's just sleeping. Nothing's going to happen to her."

She nodded solemnly. "Not while I'm taking care of her."

I should have known the house was listening.

LOOKING BACK, I'M certain it only took me a few minutes to slip out of my morning dress and into something dry. I can remember the soft whuffle of the fabric as it slid over my head. I remember taking a moment to towel my hair and smooth out the points of my collar. But how long could that have taken? Five minutes? Six, if I combed my hair? Did I rub lotion into my chapped knuckles, and did that add two or three minutes? My stockings were the worst, I remember that. They clung to my damp legs like barnacles to rocks.

Still, it could not have taken me more than fifteen minutes to change and dry and pull myself together. It shouldn't have been enough time to ruin everything, and yet it was.

TWELVE

T HE DOORS WERE all open. Frederick's old room, the spare
bedroom, the empty room that should have been Abigail's:
all the way from one end of the hall to the other, the doors stood
open and silent.

"Abigail?"

I could just hear the tinny recording of a piano filtering up
from the floor below. Frederick must have been listening to the
gramophone in his study.

"Lillian?"

My knees wobbled a little as I walked to her door. The yellow
light remained on, and the musty smell was worse, creeping out
into the hall. The covers had wadded themselves into one corner
of the bed.

I backed away from the bedroom, not taking my eyes from
the door. The ottoman had been shoved aside. The door could
slam shut any moment. My heel came down on something soft
and I whirled around with a shriek.

I had stepped on Pewter's misshapen arm. I picked it up,
holding back a superstitious apology. If I hadn't stepped on it, I
would have fallen backward down the stairs.

On the landing below me, my mother's portrait knocked
against the wall, once, twice, then after a pause, one more time.

I squeezed Pewter more tightly against my chest as I crept down the stairs. I did not turn my back on the painting. That seemed important.

If I had I turned at that moment, I would have seen you, Lillian, pulling yourself across the hallway floor. Going to Frederick to confess it all.

But I did not turn.

All I saw at the bottom of the stairs was the front door, wide open, and the black-and-red matchbook laying brightly on the marble floor. You might have called to me as I ran out into the rain. But I couldn't have heard you over the rain and my heartbeat, the same fierce pounding as the shutters banging against the walls of the house.

I followed Abigail through the forest all the way to the sawmill. Of course I didn't know I followed her and not you, Lillian, but that was only because my mind had stopped working at some point, possibly the moment I saw you laying so still and pale at the bottom of the staircase. A moment's thought would have warned me that no one so ill could have gotten much farther than the front door. But thinking was beyond me, so I followed Abigail down her path, and perhaps that has made all the difference.

I saw her, for a moment, running down the trail toward the sawmill. Then I stumbled on something and fell hard, dropping Pewter. It took me a second to get back to my feet. She ran so fast.

"Abigail!"

But she didn't answer. I forced myself to a run, the shreds of my stockings twisting around my legs. I burst into the clearing behind the mill and skidded to a stop. Watson's Lincoln was parked beside the mill office.

I pounded up the stairs and inside to see him slap her across her little girl face.

I ran to her side. Her upper lip already swelled, purple and split. "You son of a bitch!"

"Language, Miss Vogel." He chuckled a little. He'd been

waiting to put me in my place since the moment I refused to shake his nasty hand.

I pulled Abigail toward me. "Are you all right, Abbie?"

A bead of sweat ran down Abigail's temple, and she brushed it away. She barely spared me a glance, her attention focused on Watson. Why had she gone after him?

The woodstove gave a crackle and pop. It should have been a comforting sound, a pleasing noise straight out of my childhood, but it made my neck hairs prickle. I glanced at the woodstove. Its sides rippled with heat.

Abigail pushed me away. "You shouldn't have said those things to my Papa. You shouldn't have tried to hurt Lillian." Her voice sounded far older than her nine short years.

He laughed. It made his cheeks go red and shiny. He was such a fat little tick of a man, sucking the juice out of my family and making it go sour. "I'm the one who introduced your papa to his new wife. I know what she is. I know how much opium she needs to get through a day."

"Stop it." I put myself between Abigail and the beast. "She was trying to get away from that life, and then you had to show up and sell her more of that stuff."

"And you know how that slut pays for it?" His vowels had gone even more Southern. "Frederick does too, no matter how much he don't want to admit it."

"Shut up."

The woodstove began to rattle. I could smell smoke.

"Or what? You'll tell Freddy to make me?" He shook his finger in front of my nose. "Unh-huh. I'm the one that runs this mill. The one who keeps a roof over your brother's fancy head. He'd be working on a fishing boat if it weren't for me, so I reckon I can say whatever I like."

My throat closed up again, all the powerlessness of my position closing around it. I knew he was right. I knew it the moment I saw the paint flaking on the French doors to the garden, the moment I saw Storm Break with only five servants, the moment Frederick had sent me the letter begging me for help. Frederick had squandered my father's legacy, and I? I was only an art teacher and a spinster.

Watson saw my weakness and pushed into it. His breath burned against my face. "Maybe you can show me a little gratitude, Miss High and Mighty. After all, I been taking good care of your brother while you ignored him in the city." His hand fastened on the curve of my buttock and squeezed hard.

"Get away from her!"

Abigail's voice roared like the sea. Watson flew backward, smashing into the searing hot stove. His coat began to smolder.

"God damn you, you little bitch!"

He lunged at Abigail and grabbed her by the shoulders. I threw myself at him, pounding him with my fists.

"Mr. Watson, I brought those papers—"

Everything went quiet as the colored truck driver stopped in midsentence, his hand still on the doorknob. Andrew looked from Watson to the battered little girl, and something in his face changed.

"You son of a bitch."

He rushed across the room and drove his fist into Watson's face. Watson stumbled into the wall.

I took a step backward, staring at Andrew in awe. What was it like to just hit somebody like that? Somebody who deserved it so much?

Watson swiped at his bloody face. "You'll pay for that, goddamnit!" He lowered his head and charged.

"No!" Abigail bellowed. She slashed her hand through the air, and Watson flew sideways again, this time his head hitting the woodstove with a horrible crunch. He fell to the floor, motionless. Smoke trickled up from his jacket.

Andrew backed toward the door, staring at Watson's motionless body. "Oh, no. Oh, no."

"We've got to get out of here. All of us." I grabbed Abigail's hand, but she dug in her heels. The thick stink of scorched wool filled the room.

"He's not dead, is he?"

Flames whooshed up over Watson's head, his oiled hair like a kerosene-soaked rag.

Andrew threw open the door. "Come on, you two. This whole place is going to catch on fire."

"Come on, Abigail!" I yanked her harder.

She stared at the burning man. "I wanted to hurt him, but I didn't want him to die."

I pulled Abigail out the door and stopped on the stairs. I wanted to cry. I wanted to double over and empty away my breakfast. I wanted to hide under a rock and escape all of this.

Andrew twitched like a man who both wanted to run and wanted to have his questions answered. "Are you okay, little girl?"

It hit me then, what would happen if he was caught here. No matter what Abigail or I said, no one would believe he hadn't hurt Watson. And yet here he was, making sure Abigail was all right.

"You better run, sir," I warned. "If anybody sees you..."

He took a step down the stairs and looked back at Abigail. "You're a strange little thing, aren't you?" Andrew said. "The strangest thing I ever saw in this town, and that's saying something."

Abigail reached out to him, then pulled back as if she thought better of it. "Thank you for helping us."

Then he was down the stairs and running down the hill toward town. I hoped he would run all the way to the train station and out of the very state of Oregon. Then I realized how strong the smell of smoke was.

I pulled Abigail down the stairs and toward the empty field behind the mill, running hard. But I had to know. I had to pause before we got to the woods. I took her by the shoulders. "Why did you follow him? What happened?"

"I told you I'd take care of Lillian, and then he showed up and said all those things, and then Father hit Lillian, and she cried. I didn't protect her like I promised you. I thought you'd stop loving me."

I stopped and stared at her. Black smoke wafted out the office door behind us, framing her in darkness. "That's not how love works, Abbie."

"Then why did Mommy stop loving me when she had the baby?"

She doubled over coughing, and I pulled her to me. Inside the office, an alarm bell rang. Men shouted. Wheezing, I forced us back into a run. I had to get back to the house to tell Frederick what happened before someone else did. I had to explain...

everything. Alarm bells rang out behind us as we raced through the trees.

It began to rain again, as hard as before. A mile away, I could hear the sea crashing against the cliffs of Storm Break, louder than I'd ever heard in my life.

THIRTEEN

THE RUN BACK up the driveway felt like a nightmare. My head and chest floated above my body, unmoored by the day, while my legs refused to move with any kind of grace. In the middle of the car turnaround, a shutter lay broken. The house was coming unhinged.

We stumbled inside, our wet shoes slipping on the marble entry. Someone had turned up the gramophone and the whole house shook with tin pan piano, wild music beating too hard, too fast. Mrs. Franklin stood at the foot of the staircase.

"Where have you been? You're filthy." Her voice could have been Maman's.

"In the woods," I managed to say.

Monsieur Alain appeared in the downstairs hallway. Red, no, rose, dappled the front of his apron. He held a stick of rhubarb in his fist. "Where am I? What am I doing? Where is Madame Vogel?"

"Monsieur Alain?" I had never seen him like this. He moved like someone haunted.

"I should go find her." He walked past me, his eyes glassed over. "Perhaps I should go to her," he said. "Yes, I think I shall."

"Monsieur Alain!"

But he was already walking out the front door, still holding his rhubarb.

Mrs. Franklin laughed. "They all leave sometime, you know." She took a step toward me. Her teeth showed, but it wasn't like a smile. "You can never count on anyone."

How many times had I heard that? Kneeling in the bathtub, my mother scouring my neck with a washcloth. Sitting beside her in the garden. Weeping in my bedroom the day she found my dolls kissing and so threw them all into the fire.

I can never count on you, June. You're just as worthless as your brother.

"You were born wrong, weren't you? She told me everything. All about your dirty, nasty skin and the dirty, nasty things you did with your dollies." She took another step forward. "I'm the only person your mother could really talk to. What did anyone else know about her or this house?"

"My mother's dead," I said. Franklin's expression didn't change.

Abigail squeezed my hand. "She's crazy," Abigail whispered. "The house makes everyone crazy."

I squeezed her hand back. Abigail was right, I realized. The house had worsened my brother's skin. The house had made Blanche fight with my father. The house had made my mother desperate to live like the great woman who ought to live in such an expansive place. My mother's obsession with fitting in and looking right had made my father put on that damn white robe and parade around Coos Bay in the night until he broke his ankle.

The painting on the landing shook angrily, but I ignored it and continued upstairs. "Lillian?" I called.

A wave of tar and camphor billowed down the hallway. Steam wafted from the open door of the bathroom. A soft baritone crooning came with it.

Frederick. What had the house done with him?

Abigail stopped, pulling my arm up short. "I'm scared."

The smell made an old fear twist in my stomach. I could try to understand my mother's obsessions, but I could not put aside the fears she had instilled in me.

"You shouldn't go down there, Miss." Beamon strode out of the steam, his arms full of towels. A drop of something plipped onto his well-shined shoe. "Mr. Vogel is taking a bath."

The droplet stretched thin, following the crease of his toes down into the carpet. Blood stained the wool like a dark rose.

He walked by me, head high, arms full, pushing past Mrs. Franklin who still waited at the bottom of the stairs. Monsieur Alain had left the door open. Beamon did not pause as he walked out into the storm.

Lightning filled the entryway hot white. Thunder crashed. The doors began to open and shut, open and shut, open and shut.

The walls hummed as we walked toward the bathroom.

Frederick's singing grew clearer and clearer as we stepped closer. "Honeymoon," he sang, "keep on shining in June."

I squeezed shut my eyes for a moment. He knew. No one could sing such a charming little song with so much anger if they didn't have good reason to.

The bathroom door flew open.

Lillian crouched beside the toilet. She looked paler and grayer than she had when I saw her laying on her bed, and every fiber of me wanted to run forward and pull her out of there. But I couldn't move. Once I had seen him, I couldn't take my eyes off my brother perched on the edge of the bathtub.

He wore only his underthings, his fine clothes abandoned somewhere outside the bathroom's confines. His arms ran red, his legs, too. Ointment clotted his face like tar on a roof.

Abigail made a tiny sound. I tried to block her view of him, but it was too little, too late.

"Frederick." I took a tentative step toward him. "What are you doing?"

"I'm just a copy of our father, aren't I? I've run his businesses to the ground, taken up his bad friends, bought the next model of his favorite cars, but I'm just a paper version of the man. I even had to buy my second wife!"

"You're a good man, Frederick. And our father had plenty of faults." I tried to put some conviction in my voice, but I couldn't believe the words. Not when I'd just seen a *real* good man leap to Abigail's rescue even though it put him in mortal danger in a town like this.

Abigail pushed past me to hunker by Lillian's side.

Frederick dug his fingers into his arms. "I thought a baby would change things for me. Make us a real family."

"You are a real family." It hurt me to say it, because there was no place in that family for someone like me. "Look at Abigail. She's holding Lillian. She wants to help. She wants to make this family work."

"We'll never be a real family. It's not just Abigail. It's not just Lillian." He scooped a handful of ointment from the canister on the edge of the tub. "This is all my fault."

"No!"

He brought the stinking stuff to his face, heedless of the mess he smeared across his mouth. "Did you know Blanche had the same skin we do?"

"I...suspected." Then I remembered the sketchbook. The missing pages. The one drawing of Blanche, her bare hand holding Abigail's. No wonder Blanche had torn up the book.

"Maman said it didn't matter. She said Blanche was so clean and good I'd never even notice. But when she touched me—" He broke off, laughing. "Like sandpaper." The laughter twisted in his throat, turned into a sound of pain. "But if it wasn't Blanche's fault, then it was mine. I'm the dirty one, aren't I?"

"Frederick, there's nothing wrong with you."

"*I am almost a fish!*"

"You're talking like a mad man!"

"You know how Maman tried to get rid of the scales. You were lucky, June! You and the other girls never got them like me. I'm disgusting. Barely human."

"It's just dry skin, Frederick." I could hardly speak. The stink of the camphor, the tears stinging my eyes. The door slammed shut behind me, creaked open. Lub-dub. Lub-dub. The house's pulse was rising.

"You should have seen the baby. Every inch of it covered in scales. Even its eyes."

"What?"

"The way it cried! It bled, June. It peeled in strips. Blanche had to do it."

"Do what?"

"The golden child," Abigail whispered. "She put the gold dust in a box."

"I couldn't make myself touch it," he said. "She was the one who picked up the pillow."

"That's how she killed Father!" I screamed. The truth burned in my throat as if the years of stifling it had brought it to a boil. My legs turned to jelly as something broke inside me, some crisp white balustrade of propriety that dammed my feelings from my will.

I had finally said it out loud. I was finally, finally myself and not just my mother's rule-abiding daughter. And in thinking it, I knew the house knew it, too.

The floor gave a tremendous lurch. Frederick crashed into the bottom of the tub, weeping. "I made her be a monster. Because I was too weak to be a man!"

A chunk of plaster broke off the ceiling and tumbled into the tub. The window exploded above Lillian's head.

"Come on, Frederick. We've all got to get out of here."

"No!" he bellowed. "We're all staying! You, and my brat, and my treacherous bitch of a wife! She killed one of my babies, too."

The wind shrieked through the window, tearing at my hair. "No, Frederick. Come on!"

Lillian pulled herself up. "I didn't kill our baby. It was the house."

He lunged toward her. "You were out of your head on opium, you stupid woman!"

Then the ceiling fell down on us.

I WOKE UP to Lillian dragging me into the hallway. For a moment, the only thing I could see were the bottoms of her feet, soft and sweetly pink. She made a sound of pain or maybe anger, like a growl, and as my head bumped along the floor I could see the bulging purple mess that was her ankle. She must have twisted it when she fell down the stairs that morning.

I shook myself free. "I'm up, I'm up." The world had gotten dark. I could hear the wind and the rain still pounding the house.

I got to my knees, my head spinning my stomach into waves. "Where's Abbie? Where's Frederick?"

Abigail stood framed in the doorway of the bathroom. The wind whipped her hair around her head; debris crashed and smashed inside the room. The bathtub could barely be seen beneath the wooden beams and debris. The far wall gave a groan and toppled inward.

I grabbed the back of her dress. "Abigail!"

She swiped at the air, and a heap of plaster shifted off the mound in the bathtub. I could feel her body shaking. "Papa!"

Lillian dropped to her knees beside Abbie, putting her arm around the girl's waist. "Come on, little one. We have to get out of here before the whole house collapses."

"Papa!" Abigail screamed, and the beam rose up slowly from the tub, bits of plaster and lathe rising like a cloud, spinning in the air. Drops of blood streaked up into the debris like rain gone wrong. Abigail's shaking grew worse.

"He's dead," I said, pressing my forehead to her back. "You can't save him."

Abigail collapsed on the floor. Her body began to buck and jerk. Foam bubbled up from her mouth.

"Abigail." I shook her shoulders. I didn't know what to do. Her eyes rolled white in their sockets.

"She picked up the roof," Lillian said. "Somehow. She just— she stopped it before it could crush you."

I took hold of Abigail's head. "Wake up, Abbie. Please be okay."

I remembered her then as a baby, playing peek-a-boo across the dining room table with me, the two of us giggling like two silly peas in a cozy pod. Blanche had hated it, but that never stopped either of us.

"I love you, Abbie. I love you."

She began to cry, great shaking sobs. I pulled her to my chest and rocked her. Rain breathed in on us, cold and soaking. The house groaned.

"We have to get out of here," Lillian warned. She helped me to my feet, despite her ankle. She led us downstairs.

Debris filled the entryway : a fallen chandelier, a massive roof beam, my mother's portrait all heaped together to barricade the front door.

"We can clear this." I crunched through the fallen plaster and grabbed hold of the painting. It didn't budge. I yanked harder. Nothing. "You can't keep us in here!"

The barricade shifted, pushing me back. Plaster rained down on my head.

"The sunroom," Lillian said from the bottom step. She leaned against the newel post, her grip on Abbie the only thing keeping the little girl upright. They both looked worn and tired.

I looked at her bare feet. The sunroom had windows on every wall.

"That beam's too heavy for us, even if the house would let us move it," Lillian said.

Abigail's teeth began to chatter. Lightning suddenly filled the room with shifting blue light. My mother's portrait seemed to grin at me.

"Abbie, can you move it?"

"N-no. My head hurts too much." She sagged against Lillian, who put her other arm around the girl. It had to hurt Lillian's ankle to take the extra weight.

"The sunroom," Lillian repeated. "It's the best way."

I went to them and hoisted Abigail in my arms. Her cheek felt too hot against the side of my face. "You can lean on me, Lil."

We turned into the hallway. Frederick's ragtime record had not stopped. Abigail and I had entered the foyer a lifetime ago, but still that music played on, just the kind of jolly tune that Frederick loved best. I choked back tears. This was no time to think of him.

Lillian hissed as her feet found the first glass in the hallway. I put Abigail down so I could help Lillian through the sparkling minefield of the sunroom floor. The wind blew through the room, unrestrained by walls or curtains. Broken branches littered the floor and rose petals clung to the furniture. The wilderness my family had cleared and built over had found its way inside Storm Break.

Mrs. Franklin stood there in her apron and mobcap, blocking the French doors with her body. I should have known she wouldn't leave. Of everyone, she had spent the most time in this house. Other people left—they ran errands, they took vacations.

She never did. The house had had years to work on her.

She hissed at us, her eyes darting from my face to Lillian's to Abigail's.

"Let us out, Mrs. Franklin."

"You deserve to die in this house." She slashed at me, her fingers gone to claws. "All you Vogels deserve to die in this house. You never cared for it like I did! You never scrubbed that marble floor or dusted any of your fine things. Your mother was the only one who knew what needed done around this place."

I tried to remember Mrs. Franklin before she had become a tool for this house, but before that, she was just a tool for my mother. She had never once been kind to me. She had never once been kind to Abigail or Lillian, either.

I did not need Abigail's powers to throw Mrs. Franklin out of my way. I remembered watching Andrew back at the mill office, and I drew back my fist. My whole body went into that punch.

How good it felt! It was like leaping over a tree trunk on a forest path, like wading into a wave on a blazing bright day, like kissing Lillian full on the mouth. I was made for this, for *doing* and *feeling*. There was so much more to me than just watching and sketching the poison of this world.

I snatched the keys off Mrs. Franklin's belt, unlocked the door, and stepped out into the storm.

A shutter whipped past my head, crashing into the water fountain in an explosion of splinters. Foam whipped off the raging sea, clogging the air. The balustrade groaned as a length of it crumbled over the edge of the cliff. The ground shook beneath my feet.

The French doors slammed shut behind us. I knew then that we had been driven to this spot. Herded like buffalo to the edge of a cliff.

The roses twisted around the boxwood hedges, closing us in. There was no way forward, save one narrow path to the edge of the cliff. There was no way to go back. One of the slate shingles slid off the roof, shattering at my feet.

It reminded me of Frederick's dandruff and the tiny flakes in the box Abigail had given me, the flakes that were all that remained of his infant son. Frederick had deserved better from the world. But so had Lillian. So had Abigail, and Blanche, and their baby, and even myself.

I breathed in stinging whispers of the raging sea. My heart pounded in my chest. Inside the house, the doors and windows that remained beat to the same rhythm. If I died, would that satisfy Storm Break? After all, it was my twin; I had awakened it with all my newfound feelings. The stifled rage and suffering inside me had redoubled inside the skin of the house.

I could end it all, I felt sure. I could put the house back to sleep. If I jumped off the cliff right now, I could make the roses fall back and a path appear for Lillian and Abigail. Unlike the rest of the Vogels, they could go free. I was the only one who could do it, because I knew, like Storm Break, what it meant to see and be consumed by seeing.

"I see you," I said. "But you never really saw any of us."

The shutters hesitated in their beating. I squeezed shut my eyes for a moment, my heart suddenly aching. There was so much I hadn't paid attention to when I'd lived here, when I'd been so lonely and miserable that I couldn't see that everyone else was, too. Storm Break was too lonely a place for any family to survive.

You're disgusting, the shutters thumped. *How can you even look at yourself*, the roses rustled in the wind. *You don't deserve to breathe my air*, the house grumbled, and its voice was my voice, its words the words I'd spent my whole life whispering in my heart.

My eyes flew open. Storm Break stared back at me, its windows flaring as all the lights blazed on.

How Blanche and Mother and Mrs. Franklin had cared for this wretched house! They had given the house love and devotion and perfect care. They had given it parties and laughter, fine things beneath its roof and great groups of people within its walls. They had made Storm Break into a great lady. But in the end, it was only a house. A skin made for its inhabitants. A skin to be worn or shed as needed.

The shutters picked up their pace. Hungry. Ready for another Vogel to give it their life. *Do it. Do it.*

The metal of the key ring bit into my palm. "Fuck you, house," I whispered. And I threw the keys over the cliff.

The house shrieked. Wood splintered and crashed as we picked our bloody way across the roses. The thorns pierced not only my flesh, but the shell I had built around myself, the shell that shut out not just suffering but also happiness, and care, and love. We all cried as our skins were ripped by those thorns, but I laughed a little, and I think that made the house scream louder.

The house was still screaming when we made it to the road.

YOU ASKED ME, Lillian, how Storm Break's story will end, what I will do with the place now that probate has resolved and I am its owner. I can't imagine living there. So many people were so unhappy within those walls, and the house soaked up the unhappiness like a small child with no one to soothe her fears in the dark.

I have been running from that unhappiness all my life, and because of that, I have struggled to see joy when it actually arrived. I think that's why I'm glad I dreamed of Storm Break last night. If we were still unhappy, then my dream would have been a nightmare. To remember Storm Break, its heart the dark twin of my own, could only be bad. But we are not unhappy, are we? Abigail still suffers her fits, and she misses Frederick dreadfully. But she sings and plays and goes to school, and she loves us. Yes, even you, Lillian. You know it's true.

You are happy, too. With your close-cropped hair and your workman's clothes you are happy as you never were in your fancy days. You laugh like a donkey. You tell jokes that make my cheeks burn.

And I? I don't just take commissions these days. I've begun making paintings for myself. They show that there is more to me than just eyes, and my feelings burn across my canvases. It is magic to feel like this, Lillian. It is *life*. I wish my brother could have learned to feel for something besides the smooth surface of polite society. If only he could have seen that all his life, all of Storm Break, was just pair after pair of white gloves.

Yesterday I received a message from the family's attorney. The shell of Storm Break still stands, though for how much longer no one knows. The cliffs begin at its back door now, and the wind and rain scour its interiors. No one will buy the land. The estate has become known as "Vogel's Folly."

I have decided to do something that would infuriate my mother: to donate the land and all the buildings to the state of Oregon. To let the wrong sort of people sit amongst the roses and eat their picnics beside the sea while the trees lean in around them, green and fresh and wild. Oh, how Maman and Mrs. Franklin would hate that! And how the very spirit of the place will grind its teeth and stir up the waves.

It will, you know. The place is more than just haunted. Storm Break, once a great house, is now a mad one. It was born, Lillian, the same day I was, crafted and loved by my very own parents. It was born, and it lived, and it saw everything.

Who knows what secrets Storm Break still hides, what golden motes still dance down its broken halls, what heart beats on within it? I take comfort knowing only this: that we are far from it, and that someday, it will tumble into the waves, unseeing at last.

ACKNOWLEDGMENTS

This book would have never been completed if not for the insight and encouragement of Christie Yant. Thank you, Christie, for never letting this one die.

A special thanks is due to the tireless conservation efforts of the Friends of Shore Acres (bit.ly/FriendsShoreAcres). The Storm Break estate is inspired by Shore Acres, the beautiful southern Oregon estate of shipbuilding and lumber tycoon Louis J. Simpson. While incidental details about the Simpson family were used to add realism to this novella, the Vogels are entirely a product of my imagination and their bad behavior should not reflect upon the Simpsons in any manner. After fire destroyed the family mansion, Shore Acres was purchased by the state of Oregon in 1942. You can enjoy a picnic on its grounds and remarkable gardens today.

Further thanks is due to the Oregon Historical Society and Oregon State University for research assistance, and especially for their efforts in documenting racism in Oregon's history.

As always, a thousand thank you's to the fabulous Masked Hucksters (writing group extraordinaire!) beta readers Jeffrey Petersen and Remy Nakamura, ending consultant Rachael K. Jones, and of course my fantastic, loving family.

About the Author

Wendy N. Wagner is the author of the horror novel *The Deer Kings* (2021). Her previous work includes the SF thriller *An Oath of Dogs*, plus two novels for the Pathfinder role-playing game, and over fifty short stories, essays, and poems. A Hugo award-winning editor of short fiction, she is also the editor of *Nightmare Magazine*. She lives in Oregon with her very understanding family, two large cats, and a small dog that might be a Muppet. You can keep up with her at winniewoohoo.com.

About the Press

Neon Hemlock is a Washington, DC-based small press publishing speculative fiction, rad zines, and queer chapbooks. We punctuate our titles with oracle decks, occult ephemera, and literary candles.

Learn more about us at www.neonhemlock.com and on Twitter at @neonhemlock.

www.ingramcontent.com/pod-product-compliance
Lightning Source LLC
Chambersburg PA
CBHW030647190726
48286CB00008B/2693